Elizabeth Gail
and
the trouble
at Sandhill Ranch

Hilda Stahl

Tyndale House
Publishers, Inc.
Wheaton, Illinois

Dedicated with love to
Aunt Edith and Uncle Burney
in memory of Deanie

Library of Congress Catalog Card Number 79-92965
ISBN 0-8423-0726-5 paper.
Copyright © 1980 by Hilda Stahl. All rights reserved.
First Printing, July 1980.
Printed in the United States of America.

Contents

One
Stranger in the barn

Just inside the old barn Libby clutched Ben's arm, her heart racing. "Do you think we should call Dad or Old Zeb?" she whispered urgently.

Ben frowned impatiently. "Why should we? Maybe you didn't see anyone run in here."

Libby's hazel eyes flashed. "I did too!" She lowered her voice. "Do you think somebody came to steal something from Old Zeb?" Libby looked around the old barn with a frown. What was worth stealing in here? A mouse streaked across the dirt floor and Libby clapped her hand over her mouth to hold back a scream.

"We'll look around to find out if anyone is here." Ben pushed his red hair off his wide forehead as he slowly walked down the dirt aisle.

Libby walked close to Ben, her eyes wide. Perspiration dripped down the sides of her narrow face and dampened her neck under her brown hair. Even this early in the morning it was hot. Old Zeb had told them yesterday when they'd arrived that Nebraska was always hot in the summer and cold in the winter. It was exciting for Libby to be visiting Sandhill Ranch — especially since it would someday be hers!

"No one's here," said Ben as he stopped close to the weathered gray boards at the end of the barn. "We'd better go eat breakfast and get ready for church."

"Not yet." Libby pointed to a ladder leading into the mow. "Maybe we should look up there." Her heart raced as she walked to the ladder. She wiped damp palms down her shorts, then gripped the sides of the wooden ladder. Slowly she climbed to the top. She swallowed hard. Why hadn't she let Ben go first? He was older than she was. Was someone waiting to clobber her on the head?

Hesitantly Libby stopped at the top and looked around. The mow floor was covered with old hay. Was it full of mice and rats? Heavy ropes and pulleys hung from the rafters. Light filtered from a large door at the far end. Old Zeb had told them that this barn was over a hundred years old.

Libby lifted herself onto the dirty floor and moved to make room for Ben. He motioned toward a pile of loose hay. Libby shivered as Ben walked toward the pile. He kicked into it, scattering it around, and Libby let her breath out in relief. She walked with him to another pile, then looked down, her heart almost stopping. She clutched Ben's arm and pointed to a toe of a tennis shoe. Ben looked surprised and a little scared. Suddenly he dropped onto the pile of hay, pinning down the person. Libby heard a grunt and a muffled cry.

"Pull the hay away," snapped Ben, his face red, then pale.

Libby's hands trembled as she grabbed the hay and tugged. A girl about her own age lay there, her face dirty, her brown eyes full of fear.

Ben jumped up and stared at her, his hands hanging limply at his sides.

"Who are you?" asked Libby hoarsely as the girl painfully sat up.

The girl pulled hay from her long brown hair and brushed hay off her yellow flowered cotton blouse. Long suntanned legs stuck out from cutoff blue jeans, badly frayed at the bottoms. "I thought you were my dad or that awful Nolen Brown," she said in a soft drawl.

Libby's legs suddenly gave way and she sank to the floor by the girl. Ben dropped down beside her, sitting cross-legged.

"Why are you here?" asked Ben sharply.

The girl flipped her long hair over her slender shoulders. "I had to hide for a while. Old Zeb wouldn't care if I stayed here." Suddenly the girl frowned. "You're strangers, aren't you?"

"But not runaways," snapped Ben. "Old Zeb invited us here so Libby could see the place her dad left her."

The girl's eyes widened. "You must be Elizabeth Gail Dobbs."

Libby gasped, then nodded. "Do you know me?"

"I'm Holly Davis. We live about five miles from here. My dad mailed some letters and a box to you for Frank Dobbs."

Libby asked eagerly, "Did you know my real dad? When he died he left his share of this ranch to me!"

"I knew him, but not very well. My dad liked him." Holly smiled. "Did you come to stay with Old Zeb?"

"Oh, no! I live with the Johnson family. This is Ben Johnson. And there's Susan and Kevin. And Toby. He was a foster boy but he's adopted now." Libby wanted to be able to say she was adopted too, but Mother wouldn't sign the papers saying she could be adopted. Would Holly know that she was only an aid kid? "We're staying for two weeks."

"I'll see if I can come play tomorrow. *If* I'm still alive by then!" Holly's voice broke and big tears filled her eyes.

"Can we help?" asked Libby as tears stung her eyes. She couldn't stand to see Holly so scared.

Holly quickly brushed away her tears and shook her head. "Only if the Johnson family could adopt me and get me out of here. Or adopt Nolen Brown!" Her eyes lit up. "He needs a family. Would you like another brother?"

Libby couldn't tell if Holly was teasing or serious. "Did you have a fight with him?"

Holly sighed. "We always fight! Nolen has lived with us about a month now. I can't stand him another day!"

10

Ben frowned. "Maybe he can't stand you either."

"He hates me! He hates everybody. He says he doesn't want to live on a ranch and be a cowboy. He'd rather live in Omaha in an apartment! Can you beat that? But he had to come live with us because we're his only relatives who will take him. He's lived with five other families and they all kicked him out after a week."

"Why are you running away from him?" asked Ben as he knocked a spider off his knee.

Holly hesitated. "I put a snake in his bed last night and when he pulled back the sheet it crawled toward him and scared him to death." Holly giggled, her brown eyes twinkling. "And I'd do it again! He's been asking for more than that. But now he's after me. Only he'll hurt me."

"You can't stay here forever," said Libby. What would she have done if Susan had done something that mean to her?

"Just as soon as I can I'll sneak home and stay close to Mom. Nolen won't try anything with Mom or Dad around."

Ben jumped up. "We gotta get to the house, Elizabeth."

Libby liked him to call her Elizabeth instead of Libby. She stood up and looked down at Holly. "Do you want to come eat breakfast with us?"

She shook her head. "I don't want anyone to know I'm here."

"How long will you stay?" asked Ben.

Holly shrugged. "Maybe all day."

"We'll bring you some dinner after we get home from church," said Libby.

Holly jumped up and clutched Libby's arm. "Promise you won't tell anyone that you saw me! Promise!"

Libby hesitated, then looked quickly at Ben's frowning face.

"You've got to promise! Please, please, for my safety you have to promise." Holly looked as if she'd burst into tears any minute.

Libby took a deep breath, then let it out. "I promise."

"I'll promise if you'll tell us the truth when we come back later," said Ben sharply.

Holly dropped Libby's arm and then swallowed hard. "What do you mean?"

Libby frowned at Ben. What did he mean?

"I will tell Old Zeb that you're here and he'll tell your family if you don't tell us why you're really here." Ben stood with his shoulders back, his feet apart. He was just a little taller than Libby and Holly.

Holly shivered. "I promise," she whispered. She lifted her rounded chin and her eyes flashed. "But now you have to promise!"

"I promise," said Ben softly.

Libby watched the tears form in Holly's eyes and slowly slip down her suntanned cheeks. How could they leave Holly alone?

"Ben! Elizabeth!"

Libby's head jerked around at Chuck's call.

"We're coming, Dad," shouted Ben, motioning to Libby to follow him.

Libby turned to Holly again. "We'll see you later," she whispered softly.

Holly nodded as she stepped back.

Slowly Libby followed Ben down the ladder. What was Holly's secret? Could they help her?

Two
Old Zeb's surprise

Libby wanted to grab Ben's arm and stop him long enough to ask him why he'd suspected that Holly had another secret. Chuck was talking to Ben about the ranch and Libby didn't dare ask Ben with Chuck around.

Hot wind blew sand against Libby's bare legs. The windmill squawked noisily as it turned, pumping water into the large tank for the horses. Would Holly be all right in the haymow by herself? Would she really stay there, or would she run off before they learned her secret?

Chuck slipped his arm around Libby's thin shoulders and she looked up at him in surprise. She'd been so busy thinking about Holly that she'd forgotten about Chuck.

"I can see why your dad liked Nebraska," said Chuck, smiling. His red hair was windblown, his face flushed from heat.

"I would get tired of the hot days and the hot

wind," said Libby. "Old Zeb says the wind blows most of the time."

"He's quite a character." Chuck grinned and shook his head. "He reminds me of an old-time rancher on a TV western."

"I know. I bet he had that hat of his all his life."

"I'd like a hat just like it," said Ben. "I'd look like a real cowboy."

That reminded Libby of Holly saying that Nolen Brown was angry about being thought a cowboy. Yet Ben wished he looked like a real cowboy. Libby smiled. It might be fun to be a cowgirl. Did Holly call herself a cowgirl?

"You are a long way away, Elizabeth," said Chuck, nudging Libby playfully. "Are you daydreaming?"

"Just thinking, Dad." She smiled up at him. "Thanks for bringing us to Nebraska to see my house and property and Old Zeb."

"I was very happy to bring you, Elizabeth. This was a wonderful opportunity for all of us to see a new state. This is the farthest west we've been. Who knows? Maybe next year we'll get to see the Rockies in Colorado."

Ben reached for the doorknob as he smiled over his shoulder at Chuck and Libby. "I'd like to climb the mountains and catch trout in the cold streams I read about."

Libby didn't know if she'd like the mountains or not. They were so tall! But it would be fun to visit them.

15

Smells of frying bacon and toast filled the kitchen as they walked into the large room. Vera stood at the stove, breaking eggs into a large cast iron skillet.

"You are just in time," Vera said, smiling quickly over her shoulder. Her blonde hair was pulled back in a knot at the nape of her slender neck. She looked cool and comfortable in jeans and a light yellow pullover blouse. "We'll have to eat and change to get to town in time for church."

"Where's Old Zeb?" asked Libby, looking around at Kevin, Toby, and Susan sitting at the kitchen table.

Kevin jumped up, his round face beaming. "He said he has a surprise for you, Libby. He's upstairs right now." Kevin punched his glasses back on his nose. "He sure was excited about getting it for you."

"I can't wait, Libby!" cried Susan, clasping her hands excitedly and shaking her head until her red-gold ponytails bobbed over each ear. "Oh, I wish I knew what it was!"

Libby walked slowly to the table and sat down, her legs suddenly feeling too weak to hold her. What kind of surprise would Old Zeb have for her? She wished her family wouldn't keep looking at her. It made her feel strange.

Chuck squeezed her shoulder as he walked past her. "That bacon smells delicious, Vera. Do you want me to take it up? Where's the platter?"

Libby caught her breath as Old Zeb walked

into the kitchen, a cardboard box in his hands. He looked strange without his tattered hat. A wide strip of his forehead just below his hairline was almost white. The rest of his face looked like brown wrinkled leather.

"Elizabeth Gail, I got a surprise for you, gal," he said as he set the box on a chair beside Libby. His faded blue eyes narrowed into slits as he smiled and deep laugh lines ran from the corners of his eyes to his gray hair. "Don't be scared, little girl. Just look inside."

Slowly Libby stood up. For a minute she thought she would collapse back in her chair. She saw the excitement as everyone moved closer to get a peek. She opened the flaps and lifted out a newspaper covering whatever was inside. She frowned. Bits of this and that lay in the box. What kind of surprise was this? She lifted her eyes to Old Zeb and caught him blinking tears away. What did this box of stuff mean to him to make him cry?

"It's everything Frank Dobbs, your dad, left here. All but his clothes, that is. I cleaned out his pockets and gave away the few things he had. But this I kept for you, Elizabeth Gail. I knew you'd come sooner or later. I was glad you could come now."

Slowly Libby reached inside and pulled out an odd-shaped packet with a rubber band around it. She heard her family talking and guessing what was in the box, but her entire attention was on the object in her hands.

17

"Breakfast is getting cold," said Vera in a tight voice.

"We'll eat in a minute," said Chuck.

Libby stared down at the pack of different sizes of snapshots. She could not look at these pictures with everyone watching her expressions. What if she wanted to cry? She would not cry in front of them. "I'll look them over carefully later," she said in a small voice that sounded strange to her ears. She found a pocket knife, a wallet with three dollars in it, papers that must have been important to Frank Dobbs, and odds and ends of the life of the man who was her real dad. He would never know that Old Zeb had saved the box of items for her. She thought about last winter when Miss Miller had told her that her real dad had been killed in a car accident. At the time she hadn't felt anything. Now she felt a strange sadness, a longing that she couldn't explain.

"We'll put the box away for now, Elizabeth," said Chuck softly as he helped her put away the things she'd set on the table. "You can go through this later when you're alone."

Libby swallowed hard and looked at Chuck, her new dad, with tears in her eyes. Chuck Johnson was the only dad she wanted and needed. Why had Old Zeb given her these things from a stranger? It just wasn't fair! What if Chuck was hurt? She would not do anything to hurt Chuck. She loved him! She loved all of her family. She did not need Frank Dobbs or his memory. Maybe they shouldn't have come to Nebraska. She should have written to Old Zeb and told him she didn't want the property he'd given Frank Dobbs, that he could have it back.

"What's wrong, Libby?" asked Toby, leaning against her arm and staring into her face. "You gonna cry?"

She frowned fiercely. "Leave me alone!"

"Libby," said Vera in a voice that warned Libby to watch how she spoke. "Get around the table, children, and we'll eat."

Libby watched as Chuck set the box in the corner near the back door. She didn't know if she should give the things to Old Zeb and tell him to keep them, or keep them herself. Old Zeb seemed to think it was important for her to have the things. Old Zeb had known and loved her dad for four years while he lived with him and worked his ranch. She would talk to Chuck in private about it later.

"Are you folks bound and determined to go to church this morning?" asked Old Zeb as he sat at the table between Kevin and Ben. "I thought you might like to walk out and see the sandhills firsthand."

"We'll walk out later today," said Chuck as he buttered a piece of toast. "We saw a church in town yesterday on our way here and we want to visit there today."

Old Zeb shook his head. "I just can't seem to get away from church-goin' people." He reached for the bacon and slid off three pieces onto his plate. "I got a family on the south of me and a family on the north of me who talk religion all the time. And now it seems I got a batch of 'em in my own house. They even got Frank to go with 'em a few times."

"Do you want to go with us?" asked Toby with a wide smile that showed a side tooth missing. Freckles covered his face and disappeared into his red hair.

Old Zeb jerked back. "Me? Not on your life, sonny. Old Zeb never went to church a day in his life and he ain't about to start now."

Libby looked at the man and knew that if he heard about Jesus and how much he loved him, he'd be glad to meet together with people who believed and worshiped God. Just a few months ago, on her twelfth birthday, she had accepted Jesus as her Savior. She was learning to be like Jesus and do what God's Word said to do. Maybe while they were visiting, she could tell Old Zeb that God loved him very much even if he never went to church.

Libby's glance fell on the box in the corner by the back door and she looked quickly away. She would not think about the things from her real dad until she was alone. Maybe she wouldn't look at them or think about them at all.

Three
New friends

With her pointed chin high, Libby walked up
the steps into the small church. Nobody here
knew that Mother had beat her and deserted her
several times, and that she was a ward of the
state. They'd probably known her real dad, that
he had cared enough for her to send her letters
and a box. Libby forced her hands to stay limp at
her sides. For once she wouldn't be called an aid
kid. Brenda Wilkens was almost a thousand
miles away where she couldn't cause trouble.
Libby thought about Joe Wilkens and sighed.
She missed him. Chuck had tried to find a way
for Joe to join them on the trip to Nebraska, but
Mr. Wilkens had refused to give his permission.
What was Joe doing today? With the time
difference he would already be out of church.
Did he miss her? Was he thinking about her
right at this minute when she was thinking about
him?

Susan grabbed Libby's arm. "Dad wants us to sit with them," whispered Susan.

Libby nodded as she walked beside Susan down the carpeted aisle. Susan's light green dress made her look even prettier than usual. Libby felt tall and awkward in her light blue dress. She just knew everyone was staring at them, thinking how sad it was to have a beautiful girl and an ugly girl in the same family.

Chuck and Vera were already getting acquainted with the family in the pew just ahead of them. A dark-haired, brown-eyed boy about Ben's age turned around and smiled right at Libby. She slumped down in her seat and wanted to sink right out of sight.

"I'm Mark McCall," he said with a wide smile that made him very good-looking. "This is my sister Shauna and over there is my little sister Vickie."

He spoke with the same slow drawl that Holly Davis had. To Libby he even looked a little like Holly Davis. Shauna had short curly hair and the same wide smile as she said hello. Libby figured Shauna was about fifteen and Vickie a little younger than Toby.

Libby cleared her throat and licked her dry lips. "I'm Libby and this is Susan, Ben, Kevin, and Toby." Libby saw Kevin and Toby flush with embarrassment as Vickie held out her hand to them and told them she was glad to meet them.

"We'll talk after church," said Mark, smiling right at Libby.

Libby nodded, then flushed as Susan playfully poked her in the ribs. Libby clutched her hands tightly in her lap as she peeked over at Ben. Had he noticed how Mark McCall looked like Holly Davis? Did Ben feel as guilty not telling his parents about Holly as she did? If he did he sure was hiding his feelings as he turned in the song book for the next hymn.

Thoughts of Holly Davis kept interrupting Libby as she tried to sing, then listen to the minister. Suddenly something he was saying made her sit up straight, her eyes wide, her heart racing.

"Holly Davis has been missing since early this morning," said the short, balding man who stood behind the pulpit. "Glen and Carol have asked us to please pray for God to protect their girl and send her home."

Libby looked quickly at Ben. He met her look, then turned back to the minister, his face flushed. Should they have made that promise to Holly? Oh, why hadn't they told Chuck? He would have known what to do about Holly.

Libby's legs felt too weak to hold her as everyone stood to pray for Holly. She leaned weakly against the pew in front of her, her head bowed, her stomach a hard cold lump. Could anyone hear the loud thudding of her heart? Was Ben as upset as she?

The minute church was over Libby rushed outdoors, knowing Ben was right behind her. She had to talk to him now! She was glad that

Susan had stopped to talk with Mark and Shauna. Several people had hurried to greet Chuck and Vera, so that gave Libby a few minutes alone with Ben.

The hot sun almost blinded Libby as she walked away from the church to the shade of a large tree. Hot wind blew her skirt against her thin legs. She pushed her hair away from her face and lifted startled eyes to Ben's face. "What are we going to do, Ben?"

"We have to tell! I know her parents must be scared badly." Ben twisted his fingers together until his knuckles popped.

"We can't tell, Ben. We promised!" Oh, why had they promised?

"How do we know she won't run from Old Zeb's barn to a place where no one can find her?" Ben stuffed his hands into his pants pockets and hunched his thin shoulders. The hot wind ruffled his hair as he stared in anguish at Libby.

"She knows we're going to talk to her after dinner. Let's wait that long at least before we tell anyone. If she's not in the barn when we go there, then we'll tell Dad all about Holly." Libby touched Ben's arm. "Is that all right with you, Ben?" Damp hair clung to the back of Libby's neck and around her face.

Before Ben could answer, Kevin and Toby raced up, their faces red and dripping with perspiration.

"Where can we hide?" asked Kevin, looking quickly behind him.

24

"That little girl's after us," said Toby, breathing hard.

"What girl?" asked Ben impatiently.

"Vickie McCall," said Kevin in disgust. "She keeps following us around." He slapped his forehead. "Oh, no! Here she comes again!"

Libby couldn't help but laugh as Kevin and Toby dashed away from the little girl. She was dressed in pink and white that made her look darker, and she ran toward them eagerly. She called to them, laughing gaily. Her short legs and little white shoes seemed to fly as she raced after the boys.

Abruptly Libby turned back to Ben, then stopped nervously as Susan and Mark walked up.

"The girl who's missing, Holly Davis, is Mark's cousin," said Susan. "He said she had a fight with her dad and just ran off."

Libby leaned weakly against the large trunk of the tree.

"What did they fight about?" asked Ben in a stiff voice.

Mark shrugged. "I don't know." He motioned toward a tall girl with long, light brown hair, dressed in a yellow and white skirt and blouse, who was walking down the church steps. "That's Leola Clements, Holly's best friend. My dad talked to her, but even she doesn't know where Holly is."

Libby looked quickly at Ben. Would he tell?

"Has Holly run away before?" asked Susan.

Mark shook his head. "I guess maybe Nolen

Brown had something to do with her running away. Nolen can get pretty mean."

Just then Kevin and Toby dashed up, begging for someone to hide them, and Libby sighed in relief. Ben couldn't tell now, not with Kevin and Toby there to hear.

Vickie giggled and ran to Toby. "I got you, Toby. I touched you. Now you gotta be my boyfriend."

Toby's face flamed redder than his hair as he jumped behind Susan. "Get away from me!"

Mark grabbed Vickie's arm and frowned impatiently down at her. "Vickie, will you stop teasing? Leave the boys alone. You know what Dad said!"

She laughed, showing a big dimple in her left cheek. "I like chasing them, Mark. Daddy won't care this time." Her brown eyes glowed with mischief. "I'm gonna kiss them as soon as I catch them."

"Oh, no you're not!" cried Toby from behind Susan.

"Kiss Toby, but not me," said Kevin, laughing as he ducked behind Ben.

"Stop teasing them, Vickie," said Mark firmly.

Vickie's wide mouth drooped and tears stood in her eyes. "I won't hurt them, Markie. They're bigger and stronger than me. I love them."

Susan knelt down in front of Vickie and hugged her. "Don't cry. I bet those boys like being chased just as much as you like chasing them."

"We do not!" cried Kevin and Toby together. With red faces they dashed away, disappearing around the back of the church.

Vickie giggled and ran after them, shouting to them that she was going to kiss them when she caught them.

"She'll never learn," said Mark, shaking his head. Then he laughed. "Your brothers are in trouble for sure if she catches them."

Libby liked Mark's laugh. She could tell by the way Susan was looking at Mark that she liked him too.

Ben cleared his throat and took a deep breath. Libby's heart raced. Ben just couldn't tell about Holly!

"Mark, I'm sorry about your cousin. I . . . I think she'll be all right, don't you?"

Libby gripped her hands together, while she kept her eyes glued on Mark's face.

"She'll be all right. God is protecting her. I sure wish she could get along better with Nolen Brown."

"Who's he?" asked Susan.

Libby started to answer, then clamped her mouth shut tight. Oh, dear! She'd almost given herself away.

"Nolen is a cousin on Holly's mother's side of the family. He's been kicked from family to family because nobody can handle him. Uncle Glen said living on a ranch in the middle of the sandhills would be good for Nolen, so he's living with them."

27

"Like Libby's living with us!" cried Susan, and Libby wanted to die on the spot. How could Susan say that right in front of Mark McCall?

Mark looked at Libby, his dark brows raised in a question.

Libby lifted her pointed chin and clenched her fists at her sides. "I live with the Johnson family. They are my foster family." If Brenda Wilkens had been there she would've told Mark that Libby was nothing but an aid kid, that she didn't belong anywhere.

Susan grinned at Libby. "She's our sister and we love her."

Tears pricked Libby's eyes. "I love my new family, too."

Mark frowned. "I thought you were going to stay here and live with Old Zeb."

"Where did you get that idea?" asked Ben sharply.

"From Old Zeb," said Mark.

Libby blinked. "You must be mistaken, Mark."

He shook his head. "No. Old Zeb told my dad that you and the Johnson family were coming here to help him on his place, that you were going to stay."

Libby gasped. Did Chuck know about Old Zeb's plans? Maybe Chuck and Vera would rather she stayed in Nebraska so they wouldn't have to have her in their family.

Libby turned quickly away. "I'm going to the car," she said in a tight voice. Maybe the whole
28

family was in on the plan to leave her in
Nebraska with Old Zeb. How could she live if
they did not want her?

Four
Trouble with Susan

The water felt cold and smooth as it slid down Libby's parched throat. She refilled her glass and drank again. What was keeping Ben? He had said he'd be right down, and it'd already been five minutes. Libby could hear Old Zeb telling the rest of the family something that they thought was funny. Chuck seemed to be laughing the loudest. She would not think about them wanting to leave her with Old Zeb right now. She had to think about Holly Davis. Was she still in the barn? Twice she and Ben had tried to go to the barn but both times someone had joined them. This was something they had to do alone.

Slowly she walked outdoors into the heat of the afternoon. If Ben didn't hurry she'd go to the barn alone to see Holly. Libby tugged at her suntop until it met her green shorts. She twisted her sandal in the soft, white sand. It felt hot against her toes. A bird sang in a nearby tree and a horse nickered in the pen that Old Zeb called a corral. She spun around at the sound of the back door opening and closing.

"Ben! What kept you so long?"

He frowned. "Let's get to the barn before someone stops us."

"What if she's not there?"

"I don't know! Let's go look."

As Libby ran beside Ben toward the barn she tried to ignore the sick feeling in her stomach. She heard the back door slam and looked quickly over her shoulder. "Oh, Ben! It's Susan! Quick. We have to get away from here."

"I don't think she saw us yet."

They ducked behind a shed and waited breathlessly. Libby chewed her bottom lip as she sagged against the weathered-gray boards of the shed. Maybe Susan would go back inside when she couldn't find them.

Impatiently Ben shook his head. "That Susan! She thinks she has to know everything. While I was upstairs a few minutes ago she asked me what was going on with you and me. She said she knew we had a secret about something. She said she'd find out what it is."

Libby knotted her fists. "Well, she's not going to learn it from me! We'll stay hidden from her until she gives up, then we'll go in the barn to see Holly Davis."

Slowly Ben peeked around the corner of the shed. "I don't see her. Maybe she gave up already. It's too hot to stay out for long."

Libby sank to the soft sand. Why had they walked into the barn this morning? This was a vacation for the family, not a time to be nervous and upset over a runaway girl.

Ben stood with his hands on his hips, his feet apart, as he looked down at her. "Elizabeth Gail Dobbs, we are not going to make another promise while we're here! I wish Holly Davis would have stayed home instead of hiding in Old Zeb's barn. I wish we hadn't talked to her at all!"

"I know, Ben. I know." Libby sighed unhappily.

A muffled sneeze at the side of the shed made Libby leap in alarm. Her heart dropped to her feet as she stared sharply at Ben. Together they jumped around to the side of the shed. Susan was racing toward the house, her ponytails flopping wildly.

"She heard us!" cried Libby, dashing after Susan. Oh, that bad, bad Susan! What if she reached the house and told everyone about Holly? With a sudden burst of speed Libby almost caught up with Susan. Libby lunged and caught Susan around the hips and knocked her to the sandy driveway. "Can't you mind your own business, Susan?" Libby gasped for breath as she moved off Susan just enough so Susan could sit up but not get away.

Susan glared at Libby. "I knew you were in trouble again! I could tell!" She struggled frantically. "Let me go! You almost killed me!"

32

"She did not," said Ben sharply. "You need to keep your nose out of our business."

"Just wait'll I tell on you! You'll be sorry, Ben Johnson! And Dad will probably make us go home, Libby. And I won't get to see Mark McCall ever again."

"You're the one who will cause trouble for us, Susan," cried Libby, her hazel eyes flashing. "You and your big mouth!"

"I just wanted to know what was going on!" She brushed sand from her arms. "You should've told me, Ben, when I asked you."

"If we let you talk to Holly with us, will you keep our secret?" asked Ben softly.

"She's not coming with us!" cried Libby, leaping up, her fists doubled at her sides. "I won't let her come. And if she tries to tell on us, I'll beat her up." Libby whirled around to Susan who was struggling to her feet. "I mean it, Susan. You'll really be sorry."

Ben touched Libby's arm but she shrugged away from him. She would not listen to Ben. He would try to talk her out of fighting with Susan. He would try to tell her to love Susan, not fight with her.

"Calm down, Elizabeth. Susan won't tell."

"Who says I won't?" Susan's blue eyes were dark with anger. Sand clung to her bare legs.

"I say you won't, Susan," said Ben firmly. "You don't want to make trouble for us or for Holly Davis."

"She wants to make trouble however she can."

Libby could barely keep from punching Susan in the nose.

"Girls, stop fighting right now! We have to see if we can help Holly. If you want to stay here all day and glare at each other, then go ahead. I'm going to the barn to see about Holly Davis." Ben turned and walked away, his shoulders stiff.

Libby looked at Susan, then shrugged. "I guess you can come if you want. Just don't tell anyone about it."

"I'm not a blabber-mouth, Libby," said Susan stiffly. "I can keep a secret, you know."

Libby managed a smile. She really did love Susan, but at times she made her so mad! Chuck had told her that Jesus wanted to help her control her temper. Too often she forgot to allow him to. "I'm sorry, Susan," she said in a low voice as they walked toward the barn. "I hope I didn't hurt you."

"I'm all right, Libby." Susan grinned sheepishly. "I'm sorry, too."

By the time they caught up to Ben, he was just stepping inside the old barn. After the bright sunlight, it was almost too dark to see inside the barn.

Libby followed Ben to the ladder and climbed up after him, Susan after her. Maybe Holly had gone home already. By now she would be very hungry and thirsty.

A cricket jumped on Libby's foot, then off, and her heart leaped. Susan stood close beside her, her hands clasped tightly in front of her, her blue eyes wide.

"Holly," called Ben softly. "Holly, are you here?"

What would Holly do when she saw Susan with them? Libby stepped closer to Ben.

"Holly, we're back. Elizabeth and I are back."

Libby looked around at the dusty hay and cobwebbed rafters. How could Holly stand it in such a hot, dirty place?

"I'm here," said Holly from a far, dark corner. She sounded scared and tired.

"Susan came with us," said Libby, handing Holly a small bag of food. "You don't have to be afraid of her. She won't hurt you."

Holly gasped and her eyes widened as she spotted Susan. "You promised not to tell anyone else! You promised! I didn't think I could trust you. I should've left here this morning."

Libby stepped closer to Holly. "Don't be scared, Holly. We want to help if we can. Susan wants to help." Libby remembered when she couldn't trust anyone. Sometimes it was hard even to trust the Johnsons.

"I met your cousin Mark in church this morning," said Susan softly. "He is very nice."

Holly's shoulders sagged and her bottom lip quivered.

"Everyone prayed for you to come home safely," said Ben.

"Mark showed us your best friend Leola

Clements. I could tell she was sad because you were gone," said Libby.

Holly blinked fast and rubbed the back of her hand across her nose. "I tried to call Leola but I couldn't use the phone without someone hearing me. Oh, I'd better go home right now no matter what Nolen does to me."

"How will you get home?" asked Libby with a frown.

"Walk. I'm used to walking. It won't take me long if I cut across the pasture."

"Dad would drive you if you let him," said Susan hesitantly.

Holly jumped back in alarm. "No! I'll just go home and no one will ever need to know I was here today. No one! You must never, ever tell!" She clenched her fists, her back stiff.

Libby looked quickly at Ben, then back to Holly. "Why would it matter if we said we saw you here and talked to you, if you're going home?"

Holly's brown eyes flashed. "It matters!"

"Look, Holly," said Ben firmly. "You can trust us. We'll help you if we can. We are going to be here about ten days. That would give us enough time to help you with Nolen Brown."

"Libby could always give him a bloody nose for you," said Susan with a laugh.

Libby flushed. She knew Susan said that because of the times she'd given Brenda Wilkens a bloody nose.

"Nolen would beat her until she was black and

blue all over," said Holly. "I'll have to take care of this myself." She walked slowly toward the ladder. "Maybe you could come see me sometime before you go home."

Libby rubbed her hand across her damp forehead. She tried to think of a way she could help Holly. She looked at Ben and Susan, then back to Holly. There was nothing she could do to help. Tears stung her eyes as Holly said goodbye and started down the ladder.

Five
Nolen Brown

Libby backed against the front porch of the Davis house and stared in surprise at Nolen Brown. How could Holly be afraid of that puny little kid? He was even shorter than Susan. He didn't look a thing like a cowboy, but more like a city boy out of place on a ranch in the sandhills. Had she looked that way when she'd first come to the Johnson farm?

"It must be fun living on a ranch," said Ben, smiling at the sullen boy who stood beside Holly's brother Aaron.

"Then *you* live here! I hate it!" Nolen stood with his thumbs in his back pockets, his thin chest pushed out. Libby thought he'd look more at home with a rough gang in a city slum.

Libby looked quickly at Holly and saw her flush. How could she and Ben get Holly alone? For three days Libby had been anxious about her.

Finally Old Zeb had brought them over to meet his neighbors.

"Me and Nol are gonna move away from here as soon as we can," said Aaron, standing just the way his cousin stood.

"Stop talking that way," snapped Holly, knocking her brother's hands out of his pockets. She glared at Nolen. "See what you're doing to him?"

"Shut your mouth!" snapped Nolen, swearing in a way that Libby hadn't heard since she moved to the Johnson farm.

"I'm gonna tell on you, Nolen," said Holly angrily. "You know you aren't to swear."

"Who's gonna stop me?" He stepped up to Holly as if he towered over her instead of reaching only to her shoulder. "D'ya want to try?"

Libby clenched her fists tightly. Nolen Brown made her very angry. He acted like Ross Atkins, a boy who'd lived in an apartment across the hall from her and Mother. Once he'd pushed her down the stairs and she hadn't been able to walk for several days. And he'd laughed!

Abruptly Libby stepped up to Nolen. She pushed her face down close to his. *"I'll* try, kid!"

"Libby!" cried Susan, grabbing her arm.

Libby shrugged her off while she kept her eyes on Nolen. "I *know* you, Nolen Brown. You're the little punk who goes around acting like the big gangster. When I was little I fought with a lot of kids just like you."

"And got smashed into the ground!" said Nolen with a sneer. "You don't scare me, stringbean. Just go back home where you belong."

"Elizabeth," said Ben firmly as he gripped her arm too tightly for her to jerk free. "We came to visit, not fight."

"We could play a game," said Kevin.

Libby stepped back from Nolen. She would not embarrass her family. She would try to tolerate Nolen Brown for the little time that they were here. She would not look at him even when she felt his eyes burning into her. He would try to get her. She knew that. She'd watch out for him and take care of him for good if she was forced to.

"Here's a frisbee," said Toby, holding up the round, red disc. "We could play frisbee tag."

"Let's do!" cried Holly in what seemed to Libby to be forced cheerfulness.

The sun felt hot on Libby's head as she ran with the others to the large grassy lawn. Nolen had seemed reluctant to join in, but Libby could see how much he enjoyed the running and tossing. Once when she found herself beside Holly she asked if she'd gotten in much trouble for running away.

"I'm grounded for practically the rest of my life," said Holly in a low voice. "You didn't tell about me, did you?"

"No." Libby frowned. "I wish we could help you."

40

"You can't. And please don't fight with Nolen. It'll only make it worse."

Before Libby could say anything else, the frisbee sailed toward her and she had to dodge out of the way so Ben could catch it. Ben could catch most any throw. She couldn't catch well at all. But she could toss it better than before.

Several minutes later Libby sank down with the others under a large tree. She gasped for breath as she wiped perspiration off her face.

Suddenly Aaron jumped up, a wide smile on his face. "Look who just drove in!" He raced toward the sandy driveway. "Mark!"

Libby's heart jumped excitedly as she watched Mark McCall climb out of the car with Vickie and Shauna behind him.

"I'm getting out of here," said Nolen gruffly. "I can't take this many Christians all at once." He made "Christians" sound like a dirty word and Libby had to bite her tongue to keep from yelling at him.

"I'm glad he's gone," muttered Holly, flipping her long hair over her shoulders. "Now we can have fun."

"Is he a foster kid?" asked Toby as he frowned after Nolen.

"He's my mom's nephew," said Holly, making a face. "They couldn't handle him in Omaha so he's been traveling from one relative to another. None of them could stand him." She sighed deeply. "So we have him and we can't handle him either, but Dad says with God's help he'll

41

make Nolen into the boy he should be."

That would be hard work, thought Libby. She remembered how terrible she was when she first moved in with the Johnsons. They hadn't given up on her and now she was almost as nice as Susan and Ben. She looked quickly at Ben and smiled. Nobody could be as nice as Ben. She looked at Susan and the smile faded away. Susan was staring at Mark McCall just the way Brenda Wilkens stared at Ben. Susan liked Mark! It just wasn't fair! Mark would never notice her with Susan around. Susan was short and cute and not afraid to speak up. Libby locked her fingers together. She was tall and ugly and could not get nice words out of her mouth without forcing them. And that was usually too hard to do.

Mark greeted Susan as if he was very glad to see her. Libby's heart sank. When he said hi to her she could barely speak. Was he happier to see Susan than her?

"Kevin! Toby!" cried Vickie, her cheeks flushed red, her eyes sparkling. "This is the best day of my life!"

"Why?" asked Toby hesitantly, moving closer to Kevin.

"Because you're here and I can see you and play with you!" Before Toby could move, Vickie threw her arms around his waist and hugged him tightly. Libby saw his face turn a brick red as he tried to push her away. Immediately she released him and threw herself against Kevin, hugging him.

Kevin tolerated it a while, then pushed her away.

"Leave the boys alone, Vickie," said Shauna with a short laugh. "You are scaring them."

"They like me," said Vickie, grinning happily. "I know they do."

Libby saw Kevin hide a smile, but Toby was scowling. Was he really angry or was he pretending to be because he was embarrassed? She thought of a lot of times that she had pretended to be angry so others wouldn't know she was embarrassed. Chuck had told her to be honest with her feelings. She was trying, but often it was hard.

A dog barked loudly somewhere near the barn. A cow mooed. Sounds around the ranch made Libby think of the Johnson farm. She looked around. Here the only trees she could see were near the house—the rest of the land was cleared. The blue sky stretched wide before her, seeming to fill up the whole place. If Mark McCall visited them, would he feel closed in?

"Let's play ball," said Mark, smiling. "Ben and I will be captains."

Libby waited in agony. Mark just had to call her for his team. When he chose Susan instead, Libby quickly turned away to hide the tears that stood in her eyes. Ben chose Libby and she ran to stand with him. Had he picked her because he felt sorry for her? Did he think Mark would never choose her?

Libby ran beside Holly to the open field where

a ball diamond was marked out. Was Nolen sorry that he hadn't joined in? Was he watching them have fun?

"I'm glad we're on the same team," said Holly with a warm smile. "We can beat those guys easy. Maybe not so easy since we have Vickie on our side." She shrugged. "Oh, well. They've got Toby with them. Is he very good?"

Libby shook her head. "But he's better than he was."

Ben called Libby to bat first. Just as she stood at home plate, Nolen dashed up.

"I'm the catcher for both teams." He stood behind Libby and dared anyone to make him leave. Libby clamped her mouth tightly shut. She would not say a word to him no matter how mad he made her!

Libby stood in position, ready for the pitch. Just as the ball came toward her, Nolen bumped against her so that she stumbled across the plate. The ball hit her sharply on the shoulder and she cried out in pain.

"Sorry," said Nolen. "That was an accident."

Libby dropped the bat and turned to Nolen. "You did that on purpose! I know you did. If you touch me again, you'll be sorry."

"Let's play ball!" cried Mark. "Nolen, if you can't stay out of trouble, leave the game."

"I'll get him yet," muttered Nolen loud enough for only Libby to hear. "He's been asking for it."

"Don't you dare hurt him," hissed Libby, her eyes flashing angrily.

Nolen threw back his head and laughed. "Libby loves Mark," he shouted. "Libby loves . . ."

Before he could say more, Libby's fist shot out and hit him full in the mouth. "Shut up, Nolen Brown!" Before she could hit him again Ben grabbed her. She struggled but he held her tightly.

"Stop it, Elizabeth!" cried Ben.

"I'll get you for that," said Nolen as he wiped away the blood on his lip. "I'll get you good!"

Libby stared at him in rage, wishing Ben would let her free to beat him until he couldn't walk or talk. And she could do it, too! She was not afraid of him.

Nolen turned and ran to the house.

"I'm glad he's gone," said Holly, her face pale. "Oh, Elizabeth! How could you do that? You won't be safe until you leave Nebraska."

Libby shivered. Holly was scaring her. Libby shrugged. "I can take care of Nolen Brown, Holly. Don't you worry about me!"

"I hope so," said Holly in a low, frightened voice.

Libby frowned. How could Holly be that frightened? What did she know about Nolen Brown that she wasn't telling?

Six
Summer storm

Libby stood with her hand trailing in the horse tank. The cold water felt good. She wanted to jump in but the sides of the tank were covered with moss and funny little snails. She hunched her shoulder where the ball had hit her the day before. This morning she'd noticed the spot was black and blue. She frowned. It had not been fair of Chuck to scold her for socking Nolen.

A fly clung to Libby's arm and she brushed it off. It was almost too hot to breathe. The sky was a strange shade of gray and for once the wind wasn't blowing.

Slowly Libby walked toward the pen beside the barn. She liked the word "corral" for the pen, but it was a strange word to use.

Old Zeb walked from the barn, his hat low over his eyes. He stopped beside Libby and pushed his hat back and looked thoughtfully at her. "You and me need to do some serious talking," he said in his slow drawl. He stood with his boots apart, his rough hands low on his hips. His jeans and blue shirt were stained and dirty.

"About what?" asked Libby hesitantly. Had Chuck asked Old Zeb to keep her on the ranch?

"Part of this place is yours, Elizabeth Gail. Your dad told me he left it to you. I think it's time you took care of what's yours."

"How can I? I'm not old enough to do anything here."

"Get your family to stay." He nodded, his eyes narrowed. "I could sure use you all here."

Libby frowned. "We can't stay here! Chuck has a farm and a store to run." Libby locked her fingers together tightly.

"You stay here with me. I can teach you all about running a place like this. Maybe someday I'd leave all of Sandhill Ranch to you."

Libby didn't know how she felt about that. It would be great to own a place as big as Old Zeb's, but it would be terrible to have to leave the Johnson family. "I . . . I can't stay here. I'm sorry."

Thunder rumbled in the distance and Libby jumped. She usually wasn't afraid of a storm, but today she felt different.

"You'll change your mind, Elizabeth Gail Dobbs. Mark my words! You'll stay right here when the others leave next week."

Libby's eyes widened and her heart raced. How could Old Zeb say that with such certainty? Before she could argue the point, Old Zeb walked away. What did he know that she didn't know?

Slowly she walked toward the gate. If she did stay here she would get to see Mark McCall almost every day. But she wouldn't get to see the family she had grown to love. What would her life be without the Johnsons? Oh, what was she thinking? She would not stay here! Chuck had told her to take her problems to the Lord and allow him to straighten them out.

She pressed her forehead against the top rail of the fence and quietly asked God to work everything out so she could stay with the Johnsons without hurting Old Zeb. She prayed that Old Zeb would find someone to help him do the work that he was getting too old to do.

"What's wrong, Libby?"

Libby looked up with a start. "Oh, Susan. You startled me."

"I wish we could go see Mark today." Susan leaned against the fence with a big sigh. She looked cool in her blue shorts and blue and yellow flowered suntop. Libby knew Mark would think she looked very pretty today. "Mark is so cute! And I love the way he says his words! I wish I had an accent."

Libby frowned. "You do have one, to people who live around here. They think we have the accent."

Susan giggled. "I guess you're right." She sighed again. "I'm going to marry Mark when I grow up."

"Don't be so dumb, Susan. You won't do any such thing!" Libby wanted to slap the dreamy look off Susan's face. "What if Mark doesn't want to marry you?"

Susan's head snapped up. "Don't say that! Don't you want me to marry him? Do you think he would want to marry you?"

Libby flushed and wished the ground would swallow her. "I'm going for a walk, Susan. I don't want to talk about such dumb things." Quickly she walked away before Susan could see how red her face and neck were. She would not think about liking Mark because it would hurt too much. He would never like her more than he did Susan. How could he? Susan was not an ugly aid kid who was too tall and thin with straight brown hair that wouldn't do anything but get messed up easily.

A tear slipped down her cheek and she quickly brushed it away. Why was she crying? She stumbled over a root and almost fell. She would think about Joe Wilkens. He liked her. He didn't care if she was an ugly aid kid. So *what* if Mark liked Susan better? Joe liked *her* better!

After several minutes of walking across the open pasture, Libby stopped and looked back toward the ranch buildings. The barn and house looked quite small. Was Susan still standing beside the pen dreaming about Mark? Libby rubbed perspiration off her forehead and licked her dry lips. Thunder cracked and she jumped. The storm seemed closer. Lightning flashed

49

across the wide sky. "I must get back," muttered Libby.

Suddenly a strong gust of wind whipped against Libby. Sand swirled around a spot that had no prairie grass. Libby ducked her head and walked into the wind toward the ranch. How strong the wind was! It almost blew her off her feet. A giant drop of rain hit Libby's face, then another. The sky seemed to open up and pour out rain, drenching Libby immediately. She wanted to stop and hide under something but there was no shelter except the ranch buildings.

The wind changed directions and blew icy cold against Libby's bare legs and arms. How could it be so hot one minute, then so cold the next? Would she ever reach the ranch? Pain squeezed her lungs. Chuck had told her that her Heavenly Father was always with her.

"Send me help," she mouthed urgently. "Please, Father, send me help right now." A sob escaped her and she blinked in surprise. Why was she crying? She stumbled and almost fell. Her legs seemed to weigh a ton. Sand gritted between her teeth. She shivered with cold.

Suddenly strong arms enveloped Libby and she looked gratefully up into Chuck's wet face. He smiled as he wrapped a warm coat around Libby.

"We'll walk together," he said. "You'll be just fine now."

Libby wanted to hug him and tell him how glad she was to see him but the words stayed in her mouth. She gripped his hand tightly and never wanted to let it go. She loved him and she knew he loved her. A warm feeling spread inside her. She remembered the first time she'd seen him. She'd been running away from the Johnson farm and he'd stopped beside her in his pickup and taken her for a ride. He'd talked to her a long time and she had never forgotten his encouragement or how the pickup had smelled with the batch of bananas lying on the seat between them.

"Just a little longer, Elizabeth," he said cheerfully. He'd always called her Elizabeth and she'd loved that too.

Finally they reached the house and stepped inside just as large hail stones thudded against the roof and onto the ground.

Libby's chest heaved up and down as she caught her breath. Water streamed from her, making a puddle where she stood.

"Oh, Libby, are you all right?" asked Susan in concern. "I was so scared for you. I wanted to go after you with Dad but he wouldn't let me."

Libby smiled at Susan, all her earlier anger and pain gone. Susan was her sister—practically her sister. She loved her.

"Oh, Libby," said Vera. "You'd better get those wet things off right away before you catch cold. I'm so glad you're here and safe."

"I didn't think it would storm so soon," said Libby, shivering. She felt warm inside at Vera's concern.

"I wanted to run in the rain," said Toby as he looked outdoors at the wet grass and sand.

"Not when it hails," said Kevin, punching his glasses against his nose. "We wouldn't want a brain concussion from a hailstone."

Libby laughed with her family. She looked around and thought she had the best family in the whole world. Old Zeb would not make her stay in Nebraska! Nothing he could do or say would make her willing to stay. And Mark McCall would not make her stay. She had a family and she would never, never leave them!

Seven
A box of memories

Libby slipped on dry jeans and sweatshirt, then brushed her hair. She looked around the small room that she shared with Susan, then gasped at the box sitting in the corner of the room. Slowly she walked to the box that held all her dad's memories. This would be a good time to look at the packet of pictures.

She wiped her hands down her jeans and took a deep breath. She remembered how angry she'd been because her dad had sent her a puzzle box and asked her to open it and think of him. She had not wanted to think of him. She had hated him. Chuck had helped her see that she had to forgive her dad and ask the Lord to take away all her hatred and bitterness.

Slowly Libby opened the box and lifted out the packet of snapshots. Had she really forgiven her dad for deserting her when she was three years old? Was all the bitterness gone? She waited for the pain, but none was there.

Her hand trembled as she slipped off the rubber band and removed the cardboard covering. Her breath caught in her throat at the picture of a tiny baby wrapped in a pink blanket. She knew even without reading the words on the back that it was she. How tiny she was at three days old! How ugly! Hadn't she ever been cute?

One by one she looked at the pictures of herself with her real parents, then of her dad and even one picture of Old Zeb beside two foals.

Had Dad ever wondered what she looked like after her third year? A tear slipped down her cheek and she brushed it away. It was foolish to cry now for Frank Dobbs.

She picked up his razor and wondered how it would've felt to have the chance to buy him an electric shaver for Christmas.

A knock at the door startled her. She twisted the rubber band around the pictures and set the box back in the corner. "Come in," she said in a voice that sounded strange to her ears.

Chuck smiled as he stepped inside the door. "You look much better. I don't believe that rainstorm hurt you at all."

"No. No, it didn't." She pushed her hands into her pockets. "You look all dried and warm."

"I am." He walked toward her, his eyes on her face. "What's wrong, Elizabeth?"

She swallowed hard. "Nothing," she said in a high squeaky voice.

He rested his hands on her thin shoulders and

looked down into her face. "I know something's bothering you, honey. Let's talk about it."

A tear slipped down her cheek and she quickly ducked her head. She would not cry! She had nothing to cry about.

Chuck pulled her gently against his chest. He smelled as if he'd just taken a shower. "It'll help you to talk to me, Elizabeth. I love you. I don't like to see you even a little upset."

Tears spilled down her cheeks and she wrapped her arms around his waist. She liked the way he held her and waited until the storm had passed. Finally she lifted her face and he wiped away the tears.

"I . . . I was looking at my dad's things. I wish he was here right now so I could see him and talk to him." Then she shook her head, her hazel eyes wide. "But if he were here, then he might make me live with him, and I could never leave you." She pressed her hands to her cheeks. "Is it right for me to feel that way?"

Chuck smoothed her hair away from her face. "It's a natural way to feel, honey. We are your family now. You belong to us. Your real dad has a special place in your heart. Don't feel guilty about that. Since he's not here to try to keep you himself, we won't worry about that." He kissed her cheek, then smiled. "Don't let a box of odds and ends hurt you. Look at the things, think about your dad, then look toward the future that you have with us."

Libby wiped the back of her hand across her

nose, then smiled hesitantly. "Would you like to see a picture of me when I was three days old?"

"I sure would! So would Vera. Shall we call her?"

Libby's stomach knotted. Was she ready for Vera to see the pictures? Finally she nodded. "I'll call her to see if she can come now."

Chuck squeezed her shoulder. "Good girl. She's in our bedroom."

The linoleum felt cool against her bare feet as she walked to Vera's bedroom door. Would Vera really want to see the pictures? Hesitantly Libby knocked. But the door opened immediately.

"I see you look warm and dry again, Libby," said Vera with a wide smile. "Are you hungry? We could go fix a sandwich."

Libby swallowed hard. "Would you like to look at some pictures my dad had of me when I was a baby?" asked Libby in a voice barely above a whisper. "You don't have to if you don't want to."

"Oh, but I'd love to!" She slipped her arm around Libby's waist and walked her back to her bedroom. "It must be very exciting having a chance to see some of the past that you don't remember."

Libby frowned. Was it exciting? Maybe a little. And a little scary too.

Chuck turned from looking at the rain out the window. He smiled. "This is a perfect day to look through old memories. All we need now is a bowl of popcorn with lots of melted butter on it."

56

"I'll see if Old Zeb has any," said Vera, her blue eyes twinkling. "It sounds like a great idea on a rainy afternoon."

Chuck and Vera sat side by side on the edge of the bed. Libby handed them the pictures one at a time.

"You were a darling baby, Libby," said Vera softly. "I would have loved to hold you and bathe you and feed you a warm bottle of milk. I guess I'm selfish, but I would have enjoyed having you every day of your life."

A warm, loved feeling spread through Libby. How different her life would have been if she'd been born into the Johnson family. But someday she would really belong to them. Mother would sign the permission sheet and the Johnsons would adopt her. Elizabeth Gail Johnson! When would that day come?

"Ben looked a lot like this when he was first born," said Chuck, grinning as he looked again at Libby's baby picture.

"Let me show you all the other things in the box," said Libby excitedly. As they looked through the things together, Libby suddenly thought about Nolen Brown. Did he have anything wonderful to remember in his past? Could he think about himself when he was younger without hurting so badly that he had to shut out all thoughts?

"What is it, Elizabeth?" asked Chuck softly.

She lifted her face, tears sparkling in her eyes. "Dad, can we help Nolen Brown? I feel so bad

57

for him. Nobody loves him, and he knows it. I hated him when I first saw him. I don't hate him now. I want to help him if I can. I want him to know that there is a chance for him to be happy and loved."

"I'll talk to Glen Davis to see if we can do something," said Chuck as he pulled Libby into his arms.

Vera held Libby's hand firmly. "Honey, I'm glad you want to help Nolen. I feel so bad for him. He has been hurt terribly. All his gruff, mean talk is to cover a broken heart. Maybe you can explain it to Holly so she'll have more patience and love for him."

"I don't think she'll listen to me. She hates Nolen. She's scared of him, too."

"Holly can't love him on her own, Elizabeth." Chuck stood up and walked toward the window. He turned, his face thoughtful. "You know how God is helping you to love Brenda Wilkens, Elizabeth. God can do the same for Holly. Tell her to ask God to help her love Nolen."

"I will, Dad." Libby sighed. "I wish that Nolen's parents hadn't hurt him."

"I do, too," said Vera, shaking her head. "Poor Nolen. I do think that Glen and Carol can help him. Maybe I can talk to Carol and give her a little advice."

"We'll all work together to help Nolen Brown," said Chuck.

Libby laughed excitedly. Who would have thought that today she would want to *help* Nolen

58

instead of beat him to a pulp? Nolen hadn't changed. She had. God had given her some of his compassion and love.

Wouldn't the others be surprised at her next meeting with Nolen Brown?

Eight
Hide and seek

Libby pressed her face against the backs of her hands and closed her eyes. She counted to five hundred by fives against the large tree that was "home."

Wind ruffled her hair. Yesterday's rain had already soaked into the sandy ground. Evening chores were finished, leaving Mark and Vickie free to play.

"Ready or not, here I come!" she shouted as she looked quickly around for movement of any kind. Had someone run behind the McCall house? Mark and Vickie would know all the good hiding places. Was Susan hiding with Mark to give her a chance to be alone with him even for a few minutes? Libby frowned as she walked slowly away from base. Mark had seemed very glad to see Susan again. But he had been glad to see her, too. Maybe he liked Susan and her the same.

Libby peeked around the side of an old shed, then dashed along the side to look behind it. Vickie and Kevin stood there, covering their mouths to hide their giggles. They stared in surprise at Libby. In a flash they ran toward base with Libby after them. Before they reached base, Libby touched them. "You're 'it' next game, Kevin," said Libby, laughing.

"I'll be 'it' with you, Kev," said Vickie, jumping up and down. "I know all the hiding spots."

Libby ran toward the house as Kevin agreed to let Vickie be "it" with him. What would Toby think of that?

"I see you, Ben!" Libby raced after him but he was too quick for her and reached base safely.

He threw back his head and laughed. "I planned it that way, Elizabeth. I knew you couldn't catch me."

Libby wrinkled her nose at him. "It won't always be that way, Ben Johnson. One of these days I will be able to run just as fast as you can."

"You'll be an old lady by then and won't want to." Ben dropped to the grass under a tree. "Keep trying, Elizabeth. Just keep trying."

Libby laughed as she ran around a lilac bush. Someday she would run fast enough to catch Ben. Wouldn't he be surprised?

"Toby! Where are you?" Libby waited for an answer. Toby couldn't stand to stay hidden long. She knew he was waiting and watching her right this minute, probably laughing at her. "Show me where you are, Toby!" A flash of blue caught her eye. Was Toby wearing a blue shirt? Or was that Mark? Susan wore yellow today. Libby dashed to the spot but no one was there. She frowned. She had seen someone!

She looked toward home base. Toby stood beside the tree, laughing hard. He had somehow gotten away from her. She would not let Mark or Susan get in free!

Impatiently she ran toward the machine shed. Hiding inside was against the rules. Maybe they were behind it. Was Mark watching her look? Her face grew hot and red. It was embarrassing to have looked so long without finding them. This was a dumb game! Why hadn't she told them she hated playing hide and seek? She could quit. She could walk right back to base and say she did not want to play. She sighed. She couldn't do that. Chuck had often told her that when you start something, finish it.

"When the going gets rough, don't quit, Elizabeth," Chuck had said. "Keep on trying."

She would keep on trying no matter what! She'd look for them until it got too dark to see. Where could they be?

She stopped beside the dog house where a big German shepherd was tied. He wagged his tail and barked at her. All at once she missed Rex, the black and tan collie at home. Did he miss her? Did he sit and watch the driveway for her to come back?

Libby swallowed a lump in her throat as she

turned to run back to base. A movement behind some bushes caught her attention. In a flash she ran around them, startling Susan and Mark who were looking around the other direction.

"I see you, Mark. Susan." Libby laughed as she ran to touch Susan. Mark just escaped her touch. Could she run fast enough to catch him?

He reached the base ahead of her and Susan jumped up and down shouting happily. Libby turned on her, her eyes flashing.

"Shut up, Susan! You try to catch him. I bet you can't run that fast either."

Susan's face flushed a bright red. "I could if I wanted to."

"Kevin's 'it' for the next game," said Ben, cutting into the conversation before the girls started fighting.

"And me too," said Vickie, grabbing Kevin's hand.

"Mark and I'll be 'it,' " said Susan, grabbing Mark's hand. Libby wanted to knock their hands apart.

"Kevin's 'it,' " snapped Libby. "You can be 'it' when you're caught first."

"Do you always have to spoil everything, Libby?" Susan stood with her fists on her hips, her feet apart. The sun made her red-gold hair look on fire.

"I could go in the house, Susan! I could stop playing!" Libby tried to hold back her anger but Susan made her so mad! Did Susan think Mark was her property?

"Don't quit, Elizabeth," said Mark. "I want you to play."

"So do I," said Ben. "Hurry. Let's hide."

Libby ignored the frown on Susan's face as she ran toward a large tree near the driveway. Mark had called the tree a cottonwood. Libby had noticed that most of the trees around were cottonwoods. She was glad Mark wanted her to stay in the game.

As she leaned against the tree out of sight of Kevin and Vickie, she glanced toward another tree. Someone was hiding there. Who was wearing blue today? Why hadn't she noticed? Maybe Mark had hidden by himself, not with Susan. Libby frowned as she tried to remember if Mark had worn a blue shirt.

Libby looked at the dirt road and wondered if cars ever traveled on it. She knew the road led to the main highway. How would it feel to live this far away from anyone else?

Libby turned just in time to see someone step around the tree down from her. She gasped. It was Nolen Brown! What was he doing at the McCalls'? Did they know he was here? She frowned. Mark would have said so, wouldn't he? Libby saw the look of sadness and loneliness on Nolen's face. But as he saw her, his features hardened into anger.

"Are you spying on me?" he asked with a scowl.

"I'm playing hide and seek. Are you playing?"

"You kidding?" He spit in the sand. "I'm no baby!"

She would not let him make her angry. "Have you met Old Zeb yet?"

He shrugged. "Sure."

"He needs someone to help him, especially during the winter. Would you be willing to?"

Nolen shook his head impatiently. "I won't be here that long."

"Sure you will. Holly said this is your home from now on."

"Holly's stupid!"

Libby took a deep breath. "If you do stay, would you be willing to help Old Zeb with his chores?"

"How much does it pay?" He stuffed his hands into his pockets and hunched his thin shoulders. The wind ruffled his light brown hair. Dirt streaked his face. Did the Davis family know where he was?

"I don't know if it'll pay anything. Talk to Old Zeb about it, will you? If you get a chance, that is." She knew he wouldn't do anything that sounded like an order.

"Why aren't you mad at me?" He asked the question, then acted as if he couldn't care less what the answer would be. He didn't fool Libby. She knew all about pretending and covering up.

Libby hesitated. If she said anything about God, Nolen would shut her out fast. If she said anything about love, he would probably hit her.

"I'm just not. Why be mad? We're going to be here just a few more days. I'd like them to be happy ones."

"Here come Vickie and your brother." Nolen ducked behind the tree out of sight again.

Libby waited breathlessly. Would Kevin see her? She would like a chance to talk with Nolen again.

"We see you, Libby," shouted Vickie, giggling. "We see you behind the cottonwood!"

Libby raced toward base, easily touching it before Kevin or Vickie could catch her. Toby and Susan were already in. Libby sat down beside them and wondered if Mark had run off alone to hide.

"Where's Mark?" asked Susan sharply.

Libby shrugged.

"I thought he hid with you."

"No. Maybe he wanted to hide alone or with Ben." Libby picked a piece of grass and stripped it with her thumbnail. She looked at her long fingers and remembered how often Chuck had said she had good fingers for playing the piano. It seemed so long since she'd touched a piano. Would she forget everything that Vera had taught her? Would Mark be impressed if he knew she was learning piano?

"Toby said he saw someone hiding near you, Libby." Susan glared at Libby.

She would not get angry again! "Susan, that was Nolen Brown. I do not know where Mark

66

was hiding." Libby was glad to see the anger leave Susan's face.

"What's Nolen doing here?" Susan looked around. "Why didn't he come in with you? Is Holly here too?"

"Nolen's alone." Libby brushed an ant off her leg. "Maybe he doesn't want to talk to all of us together."

"Here he comes now," said Susan.

Libby watched Nolen touch the base.

"I'm home free!" he shouted as Kevin and Vickie ran toward him.

"We didn't know you were playing," said Kevin. "It doesn't count."

"Wanna bet?" Nolen grabbed Kevin by his shirt and lifted his fist. "Does it count, fatty?"

Libby leaped to her feet. She knew how much Kevin hated to be called fat. He was just a little overweight. "Let him go, Nolen! Right now!"

Nolen looked at her with a smirk on his face. "Who says to?"

"Me!" Libby grabbed at Nolen just as he released Kevin.

"And now you're mad again, stringbean."

Libby stepped back and let her hands fall to her sides. Couldn't she keep her temper under control for even a day?

Nine
The fight

"You just go home where you belong, Nolen Brown," cried Vickie, jumping up and down.

Libby could see the danger Vickie was in because Nolen stood with his fists doubled.

"I can stay here if I want." Nolen stepped close to Vickie and Libby thought he was going to hit her.

"Pick on somebody your own size, punk," said Libby, pushing Nolen away from Vickie. "Are little kids the only ones you can fight?" What would she do if he gave her a black eye or a bloody nose?

Nolen jabbed at her, barely missing her as she leaped out of the way. "I fight stringbeans, too."

"Why can't we just play hide and seek?" asked Susan in a shrill voice. Libby knew Susan was frightened as well as angry. "Can't you leave us alone, Nolen?"

Before Libby could move, Nolen grabbed

Susan's arm and twisted it behind her back. "What'd you say, little girl?"

Susan screamed in pain and fear and Libby wanted to grab Nolen and throw him to the ground. She knew if she tried anything he'd twist Susan's arm harder and break it.

Helplessly Libby looked around for Mark and Ben. Why didn't they come help? Were they hiding so well that they couldn't see what was happening?

A dog barked, then the only sound was Susan's gasp of pain. Kevin and Toby stood on either side of Vickie, their faces white.

"I didn't mean to make you mad, Nolen," said Vickie in a tight voice. "You can play if you want. You can be in free."

Libby swallowed hard. Maybe if she apologized Nolen would let Susan go. "Nolen, I'm sorry for pushing you." She said it in a rush before she backed out. She wanted to pull out his hair and kick him in the shins.

Nolen twisted Susan's arm tighter and she cried out in pain. "What about you, little girl? Are you sorry you were nasty to me?"

"I'm sorry. I'm sorry," said Susan, whimpering.

Nolen pushed her away and she fell to the ground, her head down, tears flowing down her pale cheeks. Nolen squared his shoulders and stood with his thumbs in his back pockets. He looked right at Libby. "You tell Old Zeb that I'll be over to talk to him about working for him.

You tell him to pay me high wages or I won't bother."

Libby's heart beat faster. What if Old Zeb didn't want to bother with Nolen? Why hadn't she kept quiet? If Old Zeb turned Nolen down he was just mean enough to do something to hurt Old Zeb. Libby cleared her throat. "I'll talk to Old Zeb when we get home."

Just then Ben and Mark ran to base, asking why Kevin and Vickie hadn't found them. Libby saw the quick look they gave Nolen. She could not stand more trouble today.

"Who's 'it' for the next game?" asked Libby quickly, looking around.

"I will be," said Nolen, running to the tree. "I'll only count to a hundred by fives and whoever's not hidden is caught."

As Libby ran to hide she wondered how she could've had compassion or love for Nolen. He was mean! Who could ever love him? Libby squatted behind a low bush out of sight. She didn't want to play but she was afraid if she quit, Nolen would cause more trouble. Was Holly scared of him because she knew how mean he was? Or was there something else?

A fly buzzed around Libby's face and she shook her head impatiently. She squirmed around to get more comfortable. Finally she peeked around the bush. Nolen stood at base, whistling tunelessly. Why wasn't he hunting for anyone? What was he waiting for?

As she watched, Nolen crossed his ankles and

leaned comfortably against the tree as if he meant to stay there forever. Suddenly she knew what he was doing. Nolen planned to wait on base until everyone grew tired of hiding. Then when they came out, he'd tag them. Libby frowned and her eyes narrowed. She would do something about that! She waited until Nolen had his head turned away, then she dashed behind a tall clump of bushes where she found Toby, Kevin, and Vickie. In a low voice she explained what Nolen was doing.

"Let's go quietly and find the others," said Libby softly. "When we are all together we'll go in the house by the side door and stay in there a while. Nolen will get very tired waiting for us. It serves him right!"

Several minutes later Libby stood beside the kitchen sink with a tall glass of cold water. The others sat at the kitchen table with a plate of cookies. Just how long would Nolen wait before he grew impatient? Maybe he'd just give up and go home.

As the others talked and laughed Libby walked to the window and looked out at the prairie grass blowing in the wind. Several horses grazed there. It made Libby think of the two fillies that Old Zeb had showed her the first day they'd come to his ranch.

"This is Sunlight and that dark one's Midnight," Old Zeb had said in a proud voice. "Your dad named those two when they were first born."

Libby had stared at them with wide eyes as she remembered her dad writing in one of his letters about the two foals. Her dad had liked horses just as much as she did.

Old Zeb had wanted her to help him train the fillies. Dare she suggest that Nolen Brown work with Old Zeb? Did Nolen even like horses?

Libby turned as Ben joined her at the window.

"What's wrong, Elizabeth?" He tilted his head and studied her thoughtfully. "Are you feeling bad about the trick we're playing on Nolen?"

Libby flushed. She hadn't thought about feeling bad. Nolen deserved whatever he got. "Do you feel bad, Ben?"

He nodded. "I know that Nolen doesn't have any friends. The only one who's nice to him is Aaron Davis. I know how I'd feel if everyone ignored me all the time." Ben pushed back his hair. "Nolen doesn't know that Jesus loves him. I don't think Nolen has anyone to love him, and he knows it."

Libby nodded, tears pricking her eyes. "Let's take him some cookies."

A few minutes later Libby walked beside Ben with three cookies in her hand. Susan and Mark walked just behind and Libby heard Susan giggle at something Mark said. Libby's stomach knotted and she wanted to tell Susan to shut her mouth.

Nolen pushed himself up from the grass and glared at them. "Where have you been? I looked and looked for you."

Libby held out the cookies. "I brought you some cookies."

"We were in having a snack," said Susan.

Nolen took the cookies and one by one dropped them on the ground. He twisted his heel on them, grinding them into the grass.

"Why'd you do that?" asked Susan angrily.

"I don't want your dumb cookies!" Nolen pushed his hands into his pockets. "I don't need anything from anybody."

Libby looked at Nolen and he reminded her of herself. How often had she done something mean just because she hurt so bad inside? What had Nolen's parents done to him to cause such feelings and actions? Poor Nolen! Without Jesus to help him he could not change.

After a few minutes of silence Mark said, "Want to see the new calves?"

The others agreed but Libby said, "I want to stay and talk to Nolen a while. We might be down later." She saw the surprise on Ben's face. He opened his mouth, then closed it. She was glad he hadn't said anything. As they walked away Libby prayed for the right words to say to Nolen.

He looked at her with a frown. "Well?"

She shrugged. "Well what?"

"You gonna yell at me for smashing the cookies?" Defiantly he stared at her.

She wished that he'd drop his hard shell so she could see how he really felt. "Look, Nolen. You aren't the only kid in the world that's been treated bad. Look at the chance you have with the Davis family. You could be happy."

"Who needs to be happy? I need more action." He twisted his tennis shoe in the grass until sand showed. "I won't be staying here long anyway. I'm not made for this cowboy life."

"Can you ride a horse?"

"Me? Sure I can!" He shrugged his thin shoulders and looked down at his toes.

"That means you can't, but you don't want anyone to know." She saw the surprised look in his eyes before he could mask it.

"I can ride!"

"I know Old Zeb would teach you to ride. He wouldn't laugh or make fun of you. He could teach you a lot of things."

"He's a funny old man. I don't want him showing me how to do anything. I don't want anybody showing me anything! I know all I need to know."

Libby picked a leaf and rubbed her fingers over it. "I am a little afraid to talk to Old Zeb about you." She stopped in surprise. Now, why had she admitted that? "What I mean is . . ." She stopped again, then looked Nolen right in the eye. "I am afraid to talk to Old Zeb about you because I don't know him very well. He will get mad at me for not staying with him. He might hate me for asking him to let you help him instead of me. He said he was counting on me staying. He said my dad would've wanted it."

74

Libby locked her fingers together. How could she talk this honestly with Nolen? "Chuck's my dad now. I want to stay with him, with my new family. Old Zeb doesn't understand that."

"He's probably lonely," said Nolen in a low voice, his eyes down. "He wants someone of his own."

Libby rubbed her hand up her arm. She knew that feeling very well. In all the years that she'd been pushed from one foster home to another, she'd always wanted someone of her own, someone she could love who loved her. Nolen must feel the same way. "I wish he had someone of his own so I wouldn't have to feel so guilty. He's really old!"

"Probably at least sixty-five." Nolen leaned against the tree, his left foot against the tree, his knee high.

Libby stepped closer to Nolen. "For Old Zeb's sake, would you try to help him? Maybe your uncle would let you move in with Old Zeb."

"He'd be glad to be rid of me. I guess it would be better than juvie court." He frowned thoughtfully. "Since you're scared to talk to him, I'll do it myself. Man to man. I just might get farther doing that."

"You sure should try, Nolen."

"I wonder if he knows about . . ." Nolen stopped and Libby saw his face flush red. "Never mind." He dropped his foot to the ground. "I'm going in for a cookie. I'm hungry."

Libby watched him run to the house. What

75

had he started to say? He probably had as many secrets locked inside him as she had inside her. She sighed as she turned to watch the brilliant shades of orange and red and yellow in the western sky.

With a shout Ben and Mark ran toward Libby, Susan trailing behind.

"Elizabeth, I wish we could move here," said Ben, his blue eyes sparkling happily. "Mark gets to take a week off school in the spring for the roundup. He gets to camp out and everything."

"You stay here then," said Susan. "We could always adopt another boy." She winked at Libby. "Maybe Nolen Brown. Want to trade Ben for Nolen, Libby? It might be the best trade in the world." She doubled over with laughter but Libby didn't think it was very funny. Nolen would have been very hurt if he'd heard Susan.

Libby turned at a sound behind her. Nolen stood there, his face pale. He had heard! "I thought you went for a cookie," she said weakly.

"I came back." He stood with his hands rested lightly on his narrow hips. He looked Susan right in the eye. "What's so funny about trading me for him?" He motioned with his head to Ben.

"It's not a very good trade," said Ben. "At least not for you. You'd have to put up with my sister Susan with the big mouth."

Libby tried to think of something to say to make Nolen feel better, but she couldn't think of anything. She was relieved when Chuck called for them to get in the car to go back to Old Zeb's. At least she wouldn't have to look at Nolen. Tears pricked her eyes as she ran to the car. Would Nolen ever find the love and happiness that she had?

Ten
Strange friends

Libby reined in Sugar Babe, then twisted in her saddle as Nolen and Old Zeb stopped beside her. Nolen sat astride Peaches, a tall palomino. Old Zeb was on Charger, a sorrel.

"You're really riding well, Nolen," said Libby, smiling. "And you've only been at it two days."

Nolen looked down at his hands resting on the saddle horn. His face and arms were tanned almost as dark as Mark's. He didn't look as much like a city boy now.

"This boy is all right, Elizabeth Gail," said Old Zeb gruffly. "Me and him's gonna get along just fine."

Libby smiled with pleasure as she nudged Sugar Babe forward. A gentle, warm wind blew against her and she lifted her face to it. Old Zeb had not been angry when Nolen had talked to him. Libby hadn't heard what they'd said to each other, but Nolen had convinced Old Zeb that he would be a good worker to have around. Nolen didn't seem so set on going back to Omaha.

Sugar Babe walked around a cactus that Old Zeb called a prickly pear. Libby had dug one up for Vera to take home. She had been excited about it.

"Why do you want a cactus?" Old Zeb had asked with a frown. "I've been trying to get rid of 'em for years."

"I like the looks of it," Vera had said with a smile. "I'll pot it and set it with my other plants in the kitchen. Every time I look at it, I'll think of Nebraska."

"I hope you have better things to remember than that, missus."

Libby smiled as she remembered how embarrassed Vera had been at first when Old Zeb refused to call her anything but missus. When he talked about her to Chuck, he'd call her "the missus."

"Did I ever tell you about that big old rattlesnake that lived alongside my barn?" asked Old Zeb, slipping his hat to the back of his head.

"A real rattlesnake?" asked Nolen, his hazel eyes wide.

"Real as you please, sonny." Old Zeb looked off across the rolling hills, then back to Libby and Nolen. Libby saw the twinkle in his eyes and knew he was enjoying an audience.

"That old rattlesnake made hisself right at home. I stayed away from him and he didn't bother me." Old Zeb chuckled and slapped his

79

thigh. "One day a big bull snake came crawlin' along and spotted that rattler. Those two got into a fight and fought until all the grass was pulled up and wasn't nothin' but sand around. I stood and watched 'em, wondering who the winner would be.

"The rattler grabbed the bull snake's tail and started swallerin' him. But that bull snake wasn't taking none of that. He grabbed onto the rattler's tail and he started swallerin'." Old Zeb stopped and looked at Nolen and Libby.

"What happened?" asked Nolen, his eyes wide as he leaned toward the old rancher.

Libby waited expectantly, her hands gripping the saddle horn. She liked the sound of Old Zeb's drawl as he told the story.

"While I was standin' there watchin' them two snakes, they kept swallerin' until POOF! They swallered each other." Old Zeb laughed until tears ran down his leathery cheeks. "POOF! And they was gone!"

Nolen frowned. "Is that true?"

"True as my name, sonny."

Libby tipped her head and studied the old man. Was he teasing? Could two snakes just swallow each other that way?

"I don't believe you!" cried Nolen, his face flushed. "I think you made that whole story up!"

"Don't go gettin' mad at me, boy. You swallered that story same as them snakes done." Old Zeb slapped his thigh and laughed hard.

Libby giggled a little. She could see that

Nolen was getting very angry. "That's what Dad calls a tall tale, isn't it, Old Zeb?"

"No tail on them snakes. Nothin' on them snakes at all." Old Zeb tugged his hat low on his forehead and nudged Charger forward.

"I don't like your dumb story," said Nolen as he bumped his knees against Peaches' sides. "Keep your old stories to yourself."

Old Zeb looked back over his shoulder and grinned, showing short stubby teeth. "You're mad because you don't know a good story when you hear it. Remind me to tell you about that bobcat I wrestled."

"I won't listen to you ever again," said Nolen with a scowl.

Libby wanted to tell him not to be such a baby, but she didn't want to make him angrier.

A movement caught her eye and she watched a jackrabbit stand tall, study them a minute, then bound away, reminding her of a kangaroo. She smiled. She wished she'd had a camera to take a picture.

They rode in silence while the afternoon sun seemed to roast Libby alive. Didn't Old Zeb notice the heat? Why wasn't he sweating as much as she was?

Old Zeb stopped on top of a hill and talked in his slow drawl about the haying time, how many cattle he ran, and what he'd hoped Libby would do with him. She kept quiet and let him talk. He must know that she would not stay. He had seemed pleased that Nolen wanted to help out, maybe even stay, if he could get his uncle's permission.

The saddle creaked as Libby moved restlessly. She could not listen to another word from Old Zeb. He made her feel too bad. She nudged Sugar Babe forward. "I'm going back to the ranch."

"Wait, Elizabeth," said Old Zeb sharply.

She looked over her shoulder at him. "I won't wait. I'll see you later." She bumped her knees against Sugar Babe.

"Come back here, Elizabeth Gail!"

Anger swept over her. She would not go back and listen to him a minute longer. What was she doing? Once again she was acting out of anger. Chuck had talked to her often about that. Finally Libby turned Sugar Babe and walked back to Old Zeb.

"What is it?" she asked barely above a whisper.

"The ranch is over that way." He motioned with his head.

She flushed. "Oh." Without another word she headed for the ranch. Nolen was probably getting a big laugh because of her. How was she to know how to get back? There weren't any signs. And she couldn't read the shapes of the hills like Old Zeb did.

By the time she reached the ranch she was hot and thirsty. "I'm glad I'm not staying here!" Her arms felt too stiff to unsaddle Sugar Babe."

"Here, let me do that." Chuck lifted the

heavy saddle and rested it on the top of the fence. "You look worn out, Elizabeth."

"I am!" She wanted to tell how embarrassed she'd felt but she just couldn't. It felt wonderful to stand in the shade of the barn and rest.

Sugar Babe rolled in the dusty pen, then shook herself. Libby could tell the horse was glad to get home, too.

"How about a tall glass of iced tea?" said Chuck as he walked from the barn where he'd put the tack. "I could use one and I think you could too."

Libby licked her lips. Sand gritted between her teeth. "I sure could." She looked up at him as they walked toward the house. "Would you want me to stay here with Old Zeb, Dad?"

He stopped, his brows raised. "What are you talking about, Elizabeth? Even if you wanted to stay, you couldn't. You belong to us! We want you. The state says you must stay with us. No! You are coming home with us when we leave."

Libby laughed and hugged Chuck hard. "I'm glad!"

"I told Old Zeb that it was out of the question. Has he been talking about it to you? Has he been making you feel guilty?"

Libby stared up at Chuck. How did he always know how she felt and what she was thinking? "Part of this ranch is mine, Dad. I am responsible for it."

"Would it make you feel better to sign it back over to Old Zeb? At least, ask him about it."

Chuck pushed his red hair back off his wide forehead. The hot sun had brought out a few freckles on his face.

Libby sighed in relief. "I would like to give it back to him. He can give it to Nolen if he wants. I live too far away to help Old Zeb when he needs it."

"Ask the Lord to lead you in this matter, Elizabeth. Follow his directions. No matter what problem you have in life, always talk to the Lord about it."

Libby walked slowly beside Chuck as he talked to her. She liked to listen to his advice. He always had an answer for her. She thought of all the talks they'd had in his study at home. Often she'd been afraid to walk into his study because she knew he was going to scold her. Several times he'd just wanted to talk to her. Would she have been able to do that with her real dad if he were still alive and living with Old Zeb?

The screen door creaked as Chuck opened it. "Mom and the kids went to visit the Clements family in town. They'll be back before supper."

Libby splashed cold water over her face and patted it dry. She thankfully drank the iced tea. It felt good against her parched throat.

"This has been a very interesting vacation, Elizabeth." Chuck pulled out a kitchen chair and sat down. "We've made some good friends and seen a new state. It's very peaceful and quiet here without close neighbors and living twenty miles from town. It's strange to see wild hay, hay that no one has to plant. Each year it comes up by itself and each year the rancher mows it and stacks it to feed his stock during the winter. It's a different place from what we're used to." Chuck smiled and nodded. "It wouldn't be hard at all to adjust to this way of life. Maybe when I retire I'll move here."

"You wouldn't leave your farm, would you?" Libby felt a panic rise inside her. What would her life be without the Johnson farm? How could she live happily without the farm?

"I guess I'm just dreaming, Elizabeth. When it came right down to it, I couldn't leave my farm. There are too many memories there."

Libby sighed in relief. The farm meant security to her after years of insecurity. She could not lose that. Once again she thought of Nolen. "What's going to happen to Nolen, Dad?"

"He has people praying for him, people who want to help him. We'll believe together that he'll realize Jesus loves him and wants to help him." Chuck rubbed his finger down the condensation on the outside of the glass. "If I could, Elizabeth, I'd take every troubled child home with me. I'd give them a chance to know love and security. But I can't."

Libby sat down across from Chuck. "When I grow up, I'll do it, Dad. I'll have a big farm with a gigantic house so I can have lots of kids live with me." Libby's heart raced wildly and her eyes glowed.

"Good for you, Elizabeth." He smiled. Libby

85

liked the laugh lines that spread from the corners of his eyes to his hairline. "I know you would be able to understand those kids and love them." He leaned back in his chair. "In the meantime we'll do what we can when we can."

"I love you, Dad." Libby's eyes filled with tears.

He took her hand and squeezed it tightly. "I love you, Elizabeth."

Libby thought of all the years that she'd wanted someone to say that to her. No one had loved her before she moved to the Johnson farm. A warm glow spread inside her. She was loved! It was a miracle!

Had anyone ever told Nolen he was loved? Did anyone love him? Why was she thinking about Nolen? He always made her so mad! But he made her sad too.

A horse whinnied and Libby rushed to the window. "Old Zeb's back. I'll go help him unsaddle the horses."

The screen door slammed loudly behind her. All her weariness was gone as she ran across the yard to the barn. "Where's Nolen?"

Old Zeb looked over his shoulder. "He stayed home. We rode to the line fence and he went home."

"I'll unsaddle Peaches." Libby worked alongside Old Zeb. By the time the horses were in the pen Libby had made up her mind to talk to Old Zeb now.

She stood beside the fence and watched

Peaches and Charger. They flicked flies away with their tails. She looked up as Old Zeb joined her.

"I'd like to give my part of the ranch back to you, Old Zeb."

"What's this you're sayin'?" He stared at her, then his eyes darkened with anger. "I get it. Old Zeb's place ain't good enough for Frank Dobbs' girl. You want a nicer house with air-conditionin'. You want more property."

She reached out for him but he scowled so angrily that she dropped her hand. "It's not that at all. I can't take care of my part of the ranch. You take it back and give it to someone else. Maybe Nolen Brown."

"Maybe I'll do just that, little lady. He won't throw no gift back in my face. He'll be happy to have somethin' of his own just like Frank was. I'm glad Frank's not here to see what you're doin', Elizabeth Gail. Since you're too high and mighty to take what's yours, then you and your family can just get out right now. I don't want you on my place a minute longer."

"Can't you understand?" Libby's eyes burned from unshed tears. "I am trying to do you a favor."

"Don't do no favors for me, Elizabeth Gail Dobbs."

She stamped her foot and dust puffed onto her shoes. "I won't. I sure won't! We'll leave and be glad to!" She ran toward the house, her face flushed with anger.

Eleven
Plain talk

Libby spun around and strode back to Old Zeb. "I was never Frank Dobbs' daughter! I am Chuck Johnson's daughter! Frank Dobbs didn't want me all the years I was growing up until after you met him."

Old Zeb's eyes flashed and he stepped closer to Libby. "You don't know any such thing. You're only lookin' at it from your eyes. Do you know how lonely it is not to have no one? Do you know how it was for Frank to have a wife who went out with other men right under his nose?"

Libby gasped and covered her mouth. She had not thought that Mother had always been that way. She'd thought Frank Dobbs had made her that way.

"That's right, little girl. Be shocked to learn the true way of things for your daddy. He said he never wanted you to know about your mother.

He said she'd change." He shook his bony finger under her nose. "But did she change? Your living with a foster family sort of speaks for itself, don't it? You think too much of yourself and how you feel and hurt and you don't take the time to think how it was for Frank Dobbs."

Libby fought against the hot tears pricking her eyes. "I don't want to hear about Frank Dobbs! I am going to the house to ask Chuck to help me pack. We'll be out of here before bedtime."

"You leave that box of Frank's stuff too, Elizabeth Gail. Don't you take nothin' that belonged to my friend." Old Zeb rammed his hat down on his head and glared at Libby through half-closed eyes.

Libby doubled her fists at her sides. "I'm sorry I even came here. I don't need anything from Frank Dobbs or from you. I have a family and they are all I need."

"You just keep burying your head in the sand just like an ostrich. You don't have to think of another person but yourself."

Libby ran toward the house, tears streaming down her flushed cheeks. Old Zeb didn't know what he was talking about. She did not just think of herself and her feelings. She had thought of Nolen Brown. She had even thought of Old Zeb. How could he say those things to her?

The door slammed behind her. Warm air in the kitchen rushed at her. Smells of perked coffee drifted through the room. She gulped for air and fought to stop the tears. She looked up through watery eyes as Chuck walked into the room.

"We have to leave."

"What?" He frowned as he walked toward Libby.

"Old Zeb said we have to leave now. He doesn't want us here any longer." Her chest rose and fell. She pressed her hands tightly together in front of her. "I hate it here! I want to go home!"

Chuck gripped her arms. "Calm down and tell me what happened!"

She struggled, trying to free herself. "Let me go! Let me go right now!" Her breath came in short, sharp gasps that hurt her throat. She had to get away by herself where no one could hurt her.

"Elizabeth," said Chuck firmly as he tightened his grip and pulled her close. "Elizabeth, I'm right here to help you. I know something hurt you, something upset you. I know your anger is only a coverup. I want to help you. I love you. You aren't alone anymore. You won't be alone ever again."

The words seemed to come from far away, but finally Libby heard them and stopped struggling. Weakly she leaned against Chuck, great sobs tearing at her throat. Gradually the tears stopped and she gulped twice.

"There, honey. Now, tell me what happened." Chuck held her away from him as he wiped away her tears.

"He was mad because I wanted to give back the ranch."

"Old Zeb was?"

She nodded as she wiped the back of her hand across her nose. "He said I thought I was too good to take anything from my real dad and from him."

Chuck brushed her hair away from her face. "We know that's not true. We know you wanted to return it because you couldn't be responsible for it at this time."

"I . . . I yelled at him." She searched Chuck's face to see any sign of disapproval. His eyes looked back at her with love and understanding.

"I think it must be very important to Old Zeb for you to have this property. I think we should talk to him together and tell him that if he wants you to have it that much, you'll be glad to keep it."

She nodded, then looked down. "I . . . I have to tell him I'm sorry for talking to him the way I did. It's so hard to remember to be polite and nice!"

"You're learning, Elizabeth. It takes time to retrain yourself. For eleven years you've been allowed to talk back to anyone in authority or to anyone who disagrees with you. I think you're doing great. With the Lord's help, you'll do even better."

She took his hand and tugged him toward the door. "Let's find Old Zeb and talk to him this minute." Her heart raced and she wondered if she'd have the courage to walk across the yard to Old Zeb. She would not back out! She would talk to him right now before she lost any courage she might have. She squeezed Chuck's hand. Oh, it was wonderful having him beside her!

"We'll do this together with the Lord helping us," said Chuck.

Libby smiled up at him as the wind blew against them. The sun felt hot against Libby's head and she was glad to get in the shade of the barn. Her stomach tightened in a hard knot as Old Zeb stepped from the barn. He saw them and turned away.

"Wait," said Libby softly. "I came to apologize."

He turned in surprise. "You don't say!"

"I'm sorry for yelling at you, for getting angry." She twisted her fingers together. "I do like this place. I do want the gift that my dad gave me. If it's all right with you, I'd like to keep it." She waited tensely as he studied her thoughtfully.

"Elizabeth wanted to make things better for you, Old Zeb," said Chuck. "She didn't know that it was important to you that she keep this place."

"It's important," he said gruffly. "It's mighty important."

Libby sat down on a wooden bench and looked up at Old Zeb. "Why is it that important?"

He sat beside her as Chuck leaned against the doorway. A horse nickered.

"Why did you think it was better for me if you gave it back?" Old Zeb pushed his old hat to the back of his head. Wisps of gray hair hung loose.

"I can't stay here to help you. I can't pay you to take care of it."

"Did I ask you to, little girl? Did I once say a thing that way? I hay your land. I run my cattle on it. If it's all the same to you, I could rent out your house."

Libby sighed in relief. "You do whatever you want."

"And I'll open an account for you and put the money in there that is fairly yours."

She gasped, her eyes wide. She looked at Chuck and he smiled.

"It won't amount to a lot, but it'll be some." He brushed a fly away. "Frank would want you to do it this way."

Libby touched the old man's bony hand. "Why is it so important to you that I keep this place? Why did you give it to my dad?"

Old Zeb rubbed his hand across his cheek. "Frank came here and helped me when I needed help. We got to be friends. He stuck by me even when I got mad and cussed at him and told him to leave. I got sick and he doctored me and done all the work hisself." He blinked hard and knuckled tears from his eyes. "He was a son to me. It took him a long time to talk about hisself, but when he did, nothing could shut him up."

Old Zeb took Libby's hand and held it. "He was mighty sorry he walked out on you. He wanted you more than anythin'. When I gave him part of my place he couldn't wait to sign it over to you. He wanted to give you somethin' that was important to him. He never owned a place of his own until I gave him this. If he was alive today he'd want you right here with him. He dreamed about it, talked about it a lot."

Libby squirmed in agitation. She didn't like to hear what Old Zeb was saying.

"We must think of Elizabeth's life the way it is now," said Chuck in a kind but firm voice. "She has us for a family now. Frank Dobbs is dead. He has no influence over her life."

Old Zeb hopped to his feet. "I know he would've wanted her to stay here with me. I know that as well as I know Frank."

Libby jumped up too and looked Old Zeb right in the eye. "I have lived in a lot of foster homes. Nobody cared about me. The Johnsons heard about me from Miss Miller, my case worker, and they prayed me into their family. God answered for them. I was mean and made a lot of trouble for them but they kept me and loved me. They taught me about God. I didn't know that Jesus loved me, that he died on the cross for me. He's alive in heaven and he loves me." Tears slipped down Libby's cheeks and she pressed her hands to her heart. "I have learned to love the Johnson family and to love God. I learned to pray and God answers my prayers! I can't leave my new family. I can't live with you no matter how much you loved my real dad, no matter how much he would've wanted me here."

"I just didn't understand, little girl," said Old Zeb in a husky voice. "I reckon I was the one who looked at only myself and thought about only me."

"Nolen Brown needs you and you need him." Libby brushed tears off her cheeks. "Nolen doesn't have anyone to love him."

"I'm gonna talk to Glen Davis and see if the boy can't stay with me even part of the time." Old Zeb shook his head. "I don't know why you should be concerned about that boy. He's caused you plenty of trouble."

"God has put his love for Nolen in me. I want him to be happy. God loves Nolen. *He* wants him to be happy."

"I don't know about this religious stuff. I would like to help the boy and he would be a help to me too."

Chuck stepped forward. "Nolen can't trust anyone in his family. He might learn to trust you, Zeb."

Libby walked to the doorway and stood quietly as she listened to Chuck talk about Nolen's problems, and the answers to them. Did Old Zeb think it was crazy to expect God to help?

During a break in the conversation Libby quietly excused herself. She walked into the bright sunlight along the sandy driveway. She was walking on her own property. She was looking at her own house. A strange feeling passed through her.

She stopped under a tree and looked around. How far across the rolling hills was her property? She was nothing but an aid kid, but she owned some property right in the middle of the sandhills.

She looked once again at the house. A movement at an upstairs window caught her attention. She frowned. No one else was home. Who was in the house? Had Nolen Brown sneaked back over and gone inside for some reason?

Libby ran to the house, making sure the door closed quietly behind her. She'd seen someone in the room the boys shared. Cautiously Libby tiptoed across the kitchen into the front room to the stairs. She stared up the narrow steps. Taking a deep breath, she rubbed damp palms down her jeans.

"It's now or never," she whispered.

Slowly she walked up, carefully avoiding the step that always creaked. It probably was Nolen snooping around where he didn't belong. What would he find of interest here?

Outside the boys' room Libby stopped, her heart thudding painfully. What if it wasn't Nolen? What if it was a prowler?

She peeked into the room and gasped in surprise, her eyes wide in unbelief.

Twelve
Holly and Aaron

"Holly Davis, what are you doing here?" Libby stood in the doorway, her eyes wide in surprise.

Holly turned, her hair whipping around her slender shoulders. "Oh! Oh, dear!" She covered her mouth with her trembling hand.

Libby walked slowly into the small bedroom that Kevin, Toby, and Ben shared. "Why are you here, Holly?"

Tears filled Holly's dark eyes and she turned away, her head down, her long hair slipping down to hide her face. "Don't ask me, Elizabeth. I can't tell."

"You'd better tell! I'll call Dad and Old Zeb."

Holly spun around, two bright red spots on her cheeks. "No! No, no, no! You can't!"

"Hey! Calm down, Holly." Libby held out her hand, then dropped it. "I want to know why you are here, Holly. And I want to know now! I will not be put off like Ben and I were the first day we

97

met you. This time you are going to tell me exactly what's going on." Libby's stomach tightened into a hard knot. Maybe it was better not to know. Maybe she should let Holly walk out without saying a word. Libby squared her shoulders. "You will tell me what's wrong or I will call Chuck and Old Zeb. I mean it, Holly! I really do mean it!"

Holly covered her face and her body shook with tears. Libby wanted to go to her and put her arms around her but she didn't dare. She would not allow Holly to get out of talking this time.

"Tell me, Holly Davis!" Libby pulled Holly's hands away from her face. Libby's heart almost stopped at the sight of Holly's terrified face. Should she make Holly talk? Wouldn't it be better to let Holly go home and just forget about seeing her?

Holly flipped her long hair over her slender shoulders. She rubbed away her tears. "I'll tell you, but when I do you'll be sorry."

"Let's go in my room and sit down and talk." Libby's legs seemed too weak to hold her as she walked down the hall to her room with Holly beside her. Sunlight streamed into the window and Libby pulled the curtain shut. She sat on the edge of the bed while Holly sat cross-legged in the middle of the bed. Libby watched Holly trace the pattern of the quilt. Finally Holly looked up and Libby saw fear in her eyes.

"Oh, Elizabeth! I can't tell you!"

Libby took her cold hand and pressed it firmly. "Yes, you can. You sure can't keep it to yourself much longer." Libby thought of all the fear she'd lived under for years. For one minute she thought of Mother, that she could still step into her life and take her back. Quickly Libby pushed that thought aside. Just thinking of Mother made Libby know what real fear was.

Holly took a long shuddering breath. "It's . . . it's Aaron."

"Your brother?" asked Libby in surprise. How could Aaron cause that much fear?

"I'll try to start right." Holly pressed her hands tightly together. "When Nolen first came to stay with us Aaron was scared of him. One day Aaron left the gate open and let Mr. Bluster out. You know Mr. Bluster, our shorthorn bull. Aaron was scared because he knew Dad would punish him for that. Nolen found out about it and told Dad that *he'd* left the gate open. Being a city kid, Nolen wasn't expected to know better."

Holly took a deep breath and let it out. Libby watched the color flush her face, then leave it pale. "Aaron was glad that Nolen took the blame and he's been friends with Nolen ever since. What Nolen says, goes. Nolen convinced Aaron that he's taking him back to Omaha with him when he goes."

Libby frowned. "Why are you so upset? Your folks would never let Aaron go with Nolen."

"Nolen told Aaron that he'd have to prove

himself first. Aaron . . . Aaron had to . . . to steal something from Old Zeb to show Nolen he would do anything for him."

"And did he steal something, Holly?"

Holly looked down. "Yes. I didn't learn about any of this until after Aaron had already taken a hundred dollars from Old Zeb's house."

"Oh, Holly!" Libby's hand fluttered at her throat. "Did Old Zeb report it to the police?"

Holly shook her head. "He didn't miss the money. I . . . I returned it before he knew it was gone. That's what I was doing the first day you found me in the barn. I didn't want Aaron or Nolen to know that I'd heard what they'd done. I took the money without them knowing it and I returned it. I didn't want Nolen to find out what I'd done."

"Did he?"

"Yes! It was awful! He said that if I didn't leave them alone, he would take Aaron and they'd run away to Omaha or Lincoln. He said they'd lose themselves so that we'd never see Aaron again." Holly slid across the bed beside Libby. "And he would! He would take Aaron away from us. Dad loves Aaron! He's going to leave the ranch to Aaron. I couldn't let Nolen do that."

"But why are you here today?"

Holly looked quickly away. "Aaron stole Ben's pocket knife. Nolen told him he had to do it. I found out and brought it back. But I can't let them know it." She turned to Libby and clutched her arms. "I must make Nolen believe that Aaron lost the knife. You will be going home in two days and Nolen won't be able to see Ben with his knife."

"Oh, Holly. Wouldn't it be better to tell your parents what's going on? They could stop Nolen. They could make Aaron see how wrong he is."

"If I say anything to them Nolen promised to run away with Aaron even if he had to force Aaron to go. He would do it, Elizabeth! He likes hurting people. He said he knifed someone in Omaha."

"Do you believe him?"

"Of course! Nolen's mean."

"Maybe he made up that story just to make you afraid of him."

"I never thought of that. I was so scared that he'd take Aaron away. I guess I was too scared to think."

"Did you know that Jesus can take away fear and give you the right answers to a problem?"

Holly hung her head. "I . . . I don't think he would hear me. I'm not very nice some of the time."

"Chuck says that Jesus loves us so much that he wants to help us. He always hears us even if we think he is busy helping somebody more important." Libby pushed her hair away from her warm face. A fly buzzed at the window. "He loves us just the way we are, even when we aren't very nice. He wants us to tell him we're sorry for being bad, then tell him what we need."

Holly lifted her face and looked Libby in the eye. "I need Jesus to make Nolen leave me and Aaron alone."

"We need to have Jesus make Nolen and Aaron into the boys he wants them to be."

"Elizabeth, would you pray for me?"

Libby gulped. Could she pray with Holly? Chuck or Vera could, but could she?

"I know how to pray before I eat and before I go to bed, but I don't know how to pray about problems."

Not long ago Libby hadn't even known how to pray before she ate or before she went to bed. The Johnson family prayed about everything, it seemed. Libby had prayed by herself where no one could hear her. "We could pray together," Libby finally said in a low voice.

Holly nodded and Libby took Holly's hand in hers just the way Chuck did when he prayed with her.

Quietly Libby asked God to show Nolen and Aaron that he loved them very much, that he wanted to have them love him. She prayed for wisdom for Holly and help for Aaron not to listen to Nolen. As Libby prayed, she couldn't believe what she was saying. God was even helping her pray! Her heart leaped with joy. She prayed longer for the boys and for Holly. When she stopped, Holly prayed, her voice breaking with sobs as she asked God to forgive her for doing wrong and for not trusting him as she had been taught. Finally Libby thanked God for hearing and for answering, the way she'd heard Chuck and Vera do.

Just as Libby opened her eyes her bedroom door opened and Chuck walked in. She felt Holly stiffen beside her.

"I thought I heard voices," said Chuck with a smile. He looked at them and the smile faded. "Is anything wrong?"

Libby looked at Holly, waiting to see what she would say.

Holly jumped to her feet and stood with her fingers locked together, tears glistening in her eyes. "Elizabeth will tell you all about it. I must go home right now."

"See you tomorrow at the cookout," said Chuck in a bewildered voice as Holly rushed out the door. He turned back to Libby with a frown. "I could tell she needed help. What can we do, Elizabeth?"

Libby took Chuck's hand and together they walked downstairs. Libby took a glass from the cupboard and filled it with cold water. She drank thirstily. She looked at Chuck and he was studying her thoughtfully.

"Can you tell me now?" he asked softly. He sat down at the kitchen table and motioned her to a chair.

Libby carried the glass of water with her to the table. Holly had said she could tell Chuck. Taking a deep breath, she tried to tell the story just the way Holly had. When she finished, her throat felt dry again and she drank the rest of the water. She watched Chuck's face to see what he was thinking.

Chuck pushed his red hair off his wide forehead. "I'm glad you prayed with Holly. That little girl has been suffering a lot these past few weeks. It's too bad she wasn't able to trust her parents enough to tell them so they could help. Nolen probably enjoyed making her suffer."

"Holly will tell her parents now." Libby leaned forward. "God will answer and help her, won't he?"

Chuck held her hands firmly. "Elizabeth, you can always trust God to keep his word. People often let us down, but God never does. You and Holly gave the problem to the Lord. He will take care of it. We will not let unbelief stop his work. I thank God with you that he is giving Holly the courage to tell her parents what's been going on with Nolen and Aaron. I thank God with you that Glen and Carol Davis will know what to do."

Libby nodded. Listening to Chuck made her *know* that God was answering right at this minute.

Suddenly the door burst open and Toby rushed in, with Kevin and Susan close behind.

"Mom bought three chickens for us to take to the cookout tomorrow," he said. "And I get to help barbecue them!"

Susan said excitedly, "Tomorrow I'll get to see Mark again. I'm going to ask him to write to me when we go home."

104

Libby frowned. Tomorrow at the cookout she'd see Nolen and Aaron as well as Mark. Tomorrow's cookout should be exciting and maybe just a little scary.

She turned away from Susan before she got angry at the way she was talking about Mark McCall. Libby had more important things to think about.

Thirteen
The cookout

Libby breathed in the delicious aroma of barbecued chicken. Her stomach growled with hunger as she watched Toby and Vera beside the wide grill in the McCalls' backyard.

Slowly Libby walked across the yard to where Old Zeb sat talking to Chuck and Brad McCall. Had Chuck told them about Nolen? Libby's heart raced. She rubbed damp palms down her jeans as she waited for Glen Davis to join the men. Would she be able to tell by his face if he knew? She couldn't think about looking at Holly or Nolen or Aaron.

Susan ran around the house, giggling loudly with Mark beside her. Libby tried not to notice how much attention Mark was giving to Susan. To Libby's surprise Mark stopped beside her while Susan ran to join Shauna and Kevin.

"Hi," said Mark with a hesitant smile.

"Hi." She wished her feet weren't so long. Was her hair very mussed? Why couldn't she think of something to say?

"Tomorrow's your last day," said Mark. "Did Old Zeb tell you that Shauna and I are going to help him train Sunlight and Midnight?"

"No." Did that mean Nolen wasn't going to work with Old Zeb? "It would be fun to help you train them." She twisted her fingers until they hurt.

"I'll write and tell you how it's going."

Libby's eyes widened. "You will?"

He nodded. "Will you write to me?"

She nodded. Why couldn't she think of something wonderful to say? Susan would've talked about a lot of things.

"I wish you could stay longer." Mark smiled at her and her heart jumped.

"I like it here." She laughed self-consciously. "Maybe I could get used to the wind blowing all the time."

"It's not blowing right now."

Libby looked around. The leaves on the trees were almost still. The smoke from the grill drifted almost straight up. She smiled at Mark. "I didn't notice. Maybe I'm used to it already."

"Will you come again next year?"

"I'll ask Chuck." Would he want her to come? Was he asking because of her or Susan? "Maybe you could come visit us sometime."

"Maybe." He stood with his hands in his

pockets. His blue T-shirt made his arms look dark. Would he ever lose his tan? Suddenly he turned.

"Here come Uncle Glen and Aunt Carol. I hope Nolen doesn't cause any trouble tonight."

Libby held her breath as she watched the Davis family rush into the backyard. Mrs. Davis set the basket of food on the large picnic table. Finally Libby was able to look at Holly. She looked pale with dark circles under her eyes. Nolen looked as self-confident as ever.

"We'll start the ball game now," said Mark.

Libby watched as Mark ran to greet his cousins. Holly greeted him, then walked across the lawn to Libby.

"I didn't tell yet," she said in a low voice. She twisted her fingers tightly. Her hair hung in two long braids over her slender shoulders. "I didn't want to spoil tonight's cookout."

"I told Chuck. He knows God is going to answer just right."

Holly blinked fast and gnawed her bottom lip nervously.

"Don't worry, Holly. If you want, Chuck will talk to your parents. He might be able to make them understand."

Holly lifted her rounded chin. "I'll tell them, Elizabeth. I said I would and I will. I have to see that Aaron's not hurt. He's my brother and I have to take care of him the best I can."

"What's this about Aaron?"

Libby jumped as Nolen stopped beside them.

108

Libby looked quickly at Holly, then back to Nolen.

"You'll know soon enough, Nolen," said Holly stiffly. "Go play ball. I don't want any trouble tonight."

"Do you think I do?" He squared his shoulders and stood as tall as he could. "Me and Zeb got a deal on for tonight. We're both gonna be our best in a crowd of Christians."

Libby saw the frown on Holly's face. Holly probably couldn't understand how it felt to be different from everyone else. Libby twisted her toe in the grass. She knew exactly how it felt. Always she had been the odd one. She nudged Holly. "Let's go play ball." She smiled at Nolen and realized it wasn't a forced smile. "Are you going to play?"

He shrugged. "If I can be a captain."

Before they could move, Vera called to Ben. Libby watched him run to her.

"Let me use your knife, Ben," said Vera.

Libby stiffened as she shot a look at Holly's stricken face.

"This I gotta see," said Nolen with a soft chuckle that turned to an exclamation of surprise when Ben handed the knife to Vera.

Libby looked toward Chuck. He was watching Nolen. Chuck started to stand up but Old Zeb caught his arm.

"I can handle this," said Old Zeb in a firm voice. He walked toward Nolen just as he was starting to punch Holly.

Libby swallowed hard as Old Zeb caught Nolen's arm in a tight grip.

"I got some talkin' to do to you, sonny. We got some things to get straight right now."

"Let me go! I don't want to talk to you. You're nothing but a crazy old man who thinks he's a big cowboy right out of the West."

"Your words don't hurt me, sonny. Let's walk away from this crowd so we can talk without soiling anybody's ears."

Libby winced as Holly gripped her arm. They both stood and watched Old Zeb lead Nolen away. Libby turned her head as she felt someone beside her. Chuck smiled reassuringly.

"Old Zeb will know just what to say." Chuck took Holly's hand in his. "I think this is a good time to talk to your parents. They need to know."

"I'll talk to them," Holly said hoarsely.

Libby looked quickly around and was surprised to see that all activity was going on as if nothing had happened.

"I'll tell my dad first," whispered Holly as she started across the yard to where Glen Davis was pitching horseshoes with Brad McCall. "But I . . . I can't tell him while he's in the middle of a game."

Chuck patted Holly's shoulder. "Don't worry. I'll take his place. I'll tell him you need to talk to him and that it can't wait."

"All right."

Libby could tell Holly didn't want to talk to

110

her dad. "Don't forget that we prayed, Holly. The Lord will give you the strength to tell him the whole story. Remember that God is with you, is always with you."

"I'll remember." Holly took a deep breath, then walked toward her dad just as he looked her way.

Libby's throat felt tight. She wanted to go with Holly but she knew this was something Holly had to do alone.

"Hey, Libby," shouted Kevin. "Come play ball."

"Not now," said Libby. "Maybe later." She would not be able to concentrate on the ball game right now.

What was Old Zeb saying to Nolen? What would Nolen do? Libby pulled a leaf from a tree and stripped it.

"What's going on, Libby?" asked Vera as Glen and Holly walked around the house, then Carol followed. "Did you do something to upset anyone?"

Libby smiled weakly. It usually was she causing trouble. For once it wasn't. "Holly had something important to tell her parents. She wanted to wait until later but she couldn't."

"It looks very serious." Vera frowned thoughtfully, then looked at Chuck just as he tossed a horseshoe. "Chuck is really enjoying himself. I think he could settle in Nebraska without any trouble at all."

"Are you glad we came, Mom?"

Vera hugged Libby, making sure the long fork she held didn't touch her. "I'm very glad. We've met a lot of wonderful people and we've seen some beautiful sights."

"Mark wants us to come again next year." Libby looked to the open pasture where the others were playing ball. Mark was pitching. "Do you think we can?" Kevin hit the ball into left field, then ran to first.

"We'll see." Vera motioned toward the grill. "Would you like to help me? Toby deserted me for a ball game." Vera chuckled as she walked with Libby toward the grill.

Libby stood back from the heat of the grill and looked at the table full of food. She wanted to talk to Holly before time to eat or she knew she wouldn't be able to eat anything.

"Elizabeth, come here, please."

Libby looked up and saw Mrs. Davis motioning to her. Her heart sank as she slowly walked to the short woman and saw her pale face and tear-filled eyes.

"Holly told us that you know everything about our problem, Elizabeth." Libby nodded and Mrs. Davis continued. "Please go get Aaron for us. We want to talk to him right now. Bring him to the front porch, would you?"

"I will." Libby's legs felt weak as she ran to the ball diamond. Aaron would not want to leave the game to go with her.

"You can be on my team, Elizabeth," called

Mark happily. "We'll win for sure."

"I can't, Mark." She walked to Aaron and he looked up at her in surprise.

"Aaron, your dad wants you," she said quietly. "He asked me to bring you to him."

Aaron's eyes darkened and he backed away. "What'd I do now?"

"He wants to talk, Aaron. Come on." She reached for him but he jerked away.

"I can walk by myself." He marched off the field toward the house and Libby walked right beside him. She did not want to give him a chance to run away.

"Around to the front porch, Aaron," said Libby stiffly.

He frowned up at her. "Are *you* gonna follow me all the way?"

She nodded. "Don't worry. I won't touch you." She walked around a bush and up to the front porch. Holly sat on the step, her face covered with her hands. Mr. and Mrs. Davis stood beside the steps. They turned as Aaron walked up.

"You stay, Elizabeth," said Glen Davis.

Libby sank down beside Holly. Why did they want her to stay? Didn't they believe Holly?

"Aaron, Holly has told us the truth about what you've been doing to prove yourself to Nolen." Glen Davis gripped Aaron's arm. "Don't try to run away. We are going to talk. This is going to be settled right now!"

Libby saw the color drain from Aaron's face. Tears filled his eyes and ran down his cheeks.

"He made me steal, Dad! He made me!"

Carol Davis tipped up Aaron's face. "He didn't make you agree to the lie about Mr. Bluster, did he? You chose that, Aaron. It was wrong. It led you in deeper and deeper. Why would you even think about leaving us? We love you. We couldn't get along without you."

Aaron dropped his head. "You love Holly better. You sure do!"

Holly jumped up. "That isn't true! You're the one who's going to take over the ranch someday. You're the boy of the family. I'm only a girl."

Libby wanted to sink out of sight or cover her ears. She should not be listening to this. She stood up, then slowly walked away around the house.

Before she realized it, Chuck was at her side and she turned to him and flung herself into his arms.

Fourteen
Goodbye, Nebraska

Mark's mother rang the dinner bell and Libby jumped. How could she eat without knowing that Holly was all right?

Just then the Davises walked around the house, their arms around each other. Holly and Aaron looked happy and their parents were smiling. Libby sighed in relief. Everything seemed to be settled just right. Had they noticed that she'd left?

"Let's get in line to get our food, Elizabeth," said Chuck, slipping his arm around her thin shoulders. "I'm hungry."

She looked up at him and smiled. It was wonderful to know he was always around to help her. "I could eat everything in sight," she said.

"Here come Old Zeb and Nolen. They look as if they got a lot settled, too."

Libby's heart skipped a beat. What would Nolen do now? She saw him look at the Davis family and scowl. Did he feel as if he didn't belong anywhere? Did he want to run away from all of them? Old Zeb must have thought so because he kept a tight hold on Nolen's arm.

Libby waited breathlessly as Brad McCall thanked the Lord for the food and good friends to share it with. How long could Nolen keep his mouth shut? To Libby's surprise, Nolen quietly walked in line, filled his plate, and sat with Old Zeb to eat.

A few minutes later Libby walked across the grassy lawn with her plate heaped full and went to sit with Holly under a tree.

"You look happy," said Libby softly as she picked up a chicken thigh red with sauce.

"Oh, Elizabeth! I should have talked to Mom and Dad a long time ago. They love me just as much as they do Aaron. They are glad I'm a girl! And Aaron doesn't really want to leave. He was sorry for getting into trouble." Holly smiled happily. "We prayed together, Elizabeth. We've never done that before. I told them how you and I had prayed together. Dad said that from now on, we're going to pray as a family every day. He still must talk to Nolen."

"Did you tell him about Old Zeb wanting Nolen to live with him?"

Holly nodded. "Dad said he would check into the legal side of it. He said it might be the best thing for Old Zeb and Nolen both."

Libby sighed in relief. Everything was working

116

out just right. She could enjoy the delicious food with Holly and the others.

Several minutes later Libby sat alone while Holly went to get a piece of chocolate cream pie. Libby leaned against the tree and closed her eyes. She was too full to eat dessert. Kevin and Toby would gladly clean up her share. They were both always hungry. She jumped as someone nudged her leg.

"Oh, Susan. You startled me." Libby leaned forward and smiled up at Susan.

"What did you say to Mark?" Susan frowned angrily as she dropped to the grass beside Libby.

"What are you talking about?"

"You should know! Mark wouldn't eat with me. He said he was going to sit with Ben."

"Susan, I didn't have anything to do with that. How could I?"

"You could have told him to stay away from me. I know how jealous you are, Libby! I could see it in your face." Susan impatiently swatted away a bee.

Libby swallowed hard. She had been jealous. "Susan, I'm sorry. If Mark wants to like you best, that's all right with me." It was hard to say that. Libby wanted Mark to like her best. But she knew jealousy was not right. God didn't want her to be jealous of Susan over Mark. Silently she asked the Lord to help her release the jealousy and fill her heart with love. She managed a smile. "Don't fight with me, Susan. I love you."

Susan hung her head. "I'm sorry. I love you, too, Libby. We'll just forget about Mark!"

Libby squeezed Susan's hand and laughed. "I don't think we could do that. We both like him too much for that."

Susan giggled and flipped her red-gold ponytails back. "You're right. We just won't fight over him. We'll both like him and he can like us both."

"He said he would write to me, Susan."

"To me too, Libby! We'll both write to him."

"He and Shauna are going to help Old Zeb train Sunlight and Midnight." Libby looked across the yard at Old Zeb and she saw him watching her. "Susan, I'm going to talk to Old Zeb. Tell Holly I'll be back soon."

Libby looked for Nolen as she walked toward Old Zeb. Finally she found Nolen at the punch cooler getting a tall glass of red punch.

"You full enough, Elizabeth Gail?" asked Old Zeb with a grin as Libby sat beside him.

She nodded. "Everything was great. Did Nolen eat anything?"

"You'd think he had a hollow leg. It's going to be interestin' havin' him around the place."

"Did you talk to Mr. Davis?"

"Yup. He said he'd see to the legal end of it. But I want Nolen and he decided that he'd be happy with me." Old Zeb ran his fingers through his thin gray hair. "I lost Frank Dobbs. Now I got me Nolen Brown. The two of us will fit each

118

other just right. He needs a boss and I need somebody to boss around."

Libby leaned forward and kissed the old man's leathery cheek.

Old Zeb jerked, then rubbed his hand on his cheek. "It's been a lot of years since I was kissed. Thanks, little girl."

"Thank *you*! You were kind to my real dad. You were great to me and my new family. And now you're going to make a home for Nolen." She smiled at him through tears. "I love you."

"You love me? You love an old goat like me who's not worth anythin'?"

She grinned. "You are important to me. You are important to God. He loves you, Old Zeb. He loves you more than I do."

Tears sparkled in his eyes and he quickly rubbed them away. "I don't want to talk that religion now."

"It's not religion, but I'll stop talking. Here comes Nolen." She wanted to walk away but she sat still. "Hi, Nolen. Old Zeb told me that you're going to stay with him. I'm glad."

Nolen plopped down across from Libby. "I can leave whenever I want. I don't have to be stuck here always."

"Would you rather starve in the city?" asked Libby sharply. "Would you rather live on the streets, or worse yet, in a home for wayward boys? Would you rather be lonely and unloved like you have been so far? Don't you dare try to

119

fool me, Nolen Brown. You're glad to be right here with Old Zeb, and you know it. You just want to sound like a hotshot city kid."

"Not so loud," said Nolen, flushing. "You don't have to let the others know we're arguing again."

"Why should you care? You don't like any of them anyway. You said you didn't." Libby's eyes flashed and she leaned toward Nolen.

"He cares, Elizabeth Gail," said Old Zeb quietly. "He just gets too embarrassed to say it. He will learn. Me and him're gonna learn a lot of things together. We decided that after our long talk a while ago. We might even decide to go to church with them folks. But don't get your hopes up too much, little girl."

Libby hugged him tightly and finally she felt his arms around her. "I do love you! I'm glad you let us come visit you."

"I was mighty proud to meet the daughter of Frank Dobbs." He drew away from her and grinned. "Don't get mad at me again for calling you Frank's daughter."

"I won't." Libby smiled as she locked her fingers together. "I was his daughter."

"Don't you ever get mad because you can't live with your real family?" asked Nolen, looking down at his glass.

"Not anymore. The Johnson family prayed me into their home. They love me and I learned to love them. I am happy." But she knew she would be happier if Mother would give permission for the Johnsons to adopt her. Maybe someday! Libby looked at Nolen and he finally looked up.

"Nolen, the Davis family and Old Zeb want you. Don't close your heart to them just because you were hurt bad in the past. Forget the past and live with things the way they are now."

"Is that easy, Elizabeth?" he asked hoarsely.

"No. But it has to be that way. And it does get easier. Learn to love and trust others. I did. I still am. My Heavenly Father helps me. He is teaching me."

"Zeb says I can't make fun of that kind of talk anymore." Nolen looked quickly at Old Zeb. "And I won't, either. But it's hard."

"We'll both learn, Nolen," said Old Zeb gruffly.

Just then Holly walked up and Libby watched Nolen grow tense. Would he try to get even with Holly?

"Nolen, Dad told me that you agreed to try to stay with Old Zeb and make your home with him. I'm glad for you. I'm sorry for being mean to you. I wish the most that I hadn't kept yours and Aaron's secret. That was bad for all of us."

Libby waited, her heart racing. What would Nolen do now?

"Think careful about your answer, sonny," said Old Zeb softly as he looked at Nolen.

Nolen squirmed uncomfortably. "I was wrong, Holly. I'm sorry. Maybe we can try to be friends as well as cousins."

Libby wanted to jump up and down.

"I will try, Nolen." Holly took a deep breath and let it out. "I'll help you learn to do ranch chores if you want."

"He'll take all the help he can get," said Old Zeb with a chuckle. He clamped his hat on his head and stood up. "I think I'll go teach those guys how to play horseshoes." He started to walk away, then looked back. "Want to learn, Nolen?"

He scrambled to his feet. "I don't know if I can."

"Sure you can," said Holly with a grin. "You're not a city boy now." Holly smiled at Libby. "He isn't an angry boy now, Elizabeth. He's going to be the happiest cowboy around."

Libby smiled. Holly looked like she was the happiest girl around. Everybody looked happy, even Toby, as Vickie chased him past the table where Libby and Holly sat.

About an hour later Libby climbed into the station wagon beside Ben. She smiled tiredly. Tomorrow they'd start home.

Toby and Kevin waved out the window at Vickie. "We'll write to you, Vickie," called Kevin through the open window.

"I'll send you lots of hugs and kisses," called Vickie, jumping up and down.

Libby laughed with the others. For a minute she felt a sadness inside. Tonight they were saying goodbye to all their new friends. Tomorrow they'd say goodbye to Nebraska.

"I think we should plan on visiting again next

year," said Vera with a satisfied sigh. "I enjoyed my stay. Did all of you?"

Libby leaned against the seat as everyone tried to tell at once what they had enjoyed most. She heard Susan say she liked meeting Mark the most, but Libby didn't feel a bit of jealousy. She smiled.

"Goodbye, Nebraska," she whispered. "Goodbye, Sandhill Ranch."

"Are you sad to leave?" asked Ben softly.

"A little," answered Libby. "But I wouldn't want to stay. I belong to all of you and I go where you go. Always!"